Granite Publishing Presents

Love Notes

#4

Oregon Flame

Other novels by Sherry Ann Miller "writer of miracles." Detailed descriptions of these novels can be read at the end of this book.

The award-winning, five-book Gift Series:

One Last Gift
An Angel's Gift
The Tyee's Gift
Charity's Gift (coming soon)
The Refiner's Gift (in progress)

The historical Warwick Saga, complete in two volumes:

Search for the Bark Warwick
Search for the Warwick II

Inspirational Romance:

Gardenia Sunrise

Oregon Flame

By Sherry Ann Miller

Published by:

Granite Publishing and Distribution, LLC
868 North 1430 West
Orem, Ut. 84057
(801) 229-9023 Toll Free (800) 574-5779
Fax (801) 229-1924

Cover Design and Art: Tamara Ingram
Layout: Triquest Book Services

ISBN: 1-59936-005-5
Library of Congress Card Control Number: 2005938798

Printed in the United States of America 2006
FC Printing, Salt Lake City, UT

Oregon Flame is dedicated to
my dear neighbor,

Irma Furman

May you find eternal treasure
in our friendship, as do I.

Hugs from Sherry Ann

Prologue:

Sharelle could not see anything; her eyelids were swollen so badly that all she could feel were slits for her eyes. Blood streaked down her face, stained her arms and hands, and bubbled from between her bruised lips. Inhaling painfully, she fought for every intake of breath which came in short, raspy gasps.

Her long hair, damp and stringy from her own blood, kept getting in her way. If she had a pair of scissors, she would cut it off so that it could no longer impede her progress. Now, all she could do was move it methodically to the side of her battered body so she wouldn't lean on it with her elbow, which only tore it in bunches from her scalp as she moved upward.

Somewhere above her, she could hear cars passing by. Around her she could smell the damp earth, the green ferns, the forest's pine scent. She could taste the blood in her mouth, but she spit it out often, determined not to swallow any.

Resolved she would not die in this overgrown ravine where her family may never find her body, she continued to pull herself up, half an inch at a time, scraping her elbows and arms as her hands grasped onto ferns and blackberry bushes in her struggle upward.

Rubbing her fingers together for warmth, Sharelle realized with horror that her ring was gone. The diamond ring her grandmother had given her had vanished. Where was it? She could not remember.

For some unknown reason, she could not feel her legs or her feet. Were they even attached to her body? Sharelle worried about this, too.

But the driving force behind her actions, putting all concern for herself out of her mind, was the vision of her mother's face if her only daughter suddenly disappeared without a trace. Sharelle could not let that happen. She had no other choice but to inch herself up the side of the ravine until she reached the road. Surely, someone would find her body there. Sharelle would at least be afforded a decent burial. And her beloved mother would have closure.

Chapter One

"Stop!" Nicole warned as she pulled the butt of her forty-four Mauser hunting rifle against her shoulder and aimed the barrel directly at the intruder's head, sighting right between his wide blue eyes.

"If you'll let me explain," he said calmly, holding out a hand while taking a step toward her.

"Pretty tough to explain why a stranger is standing in my house wearing nothing but a towel and a cocky smile! I'm completely within my rights to shoot you!" she exclaimed, anger replacing any fear she had felt earlier. At first she had been terrified to find an intruder in her house. Her fear had been replaced with fury.

The man took another step across the hall threshold, his bare foot settling on the living room carpet. At that moment, Nicole knew she would have to scare him before he would believe she was dead serious about shooting him. "I'm warning you," she said, sighting in a spider on a web about ten inches above his head on the wall above the door frame, and snugging the rifle butt tightly against her shoulder. "I'm an excellent marksman."

"I believe you," he soothed, deliberately attempting to coax her into a false sense of security.

Nicole would have none of that. "Spider at twelve o'clock," she warned and with nerves of steel she aimed and squeezed the trigger of her Mauser. BANG! The deafening sound reverberated through the house. At the same instant the butt rammed against her shoulder, a bullet whizzed above the intruder's head and burrowed straight into the wall. "Hmm. High and to the right," she smiled for the first time. "Need to sight my gun a little." Nicole saw the quivering cobweb from which the spider had been dangling, its body now splattered in tiny pieces upon the web.

All color blanched from the man's face as he turned around and looked up at the shattered cobweb and the two-inch bullet hole in the wall above the door frame.

Nicole warned again, "The next bullet will take you down, I assure you."

Keeping his back to her, the man exclaimed, "You could have killed me!"

"If that had been my intention, I would have."

"What kind of maniac did Danny send me to?" he asked.

"One who expects you face down on the carpet right about now," she said, marveling how calm her voice sounded even though her angry heart was pounding furiously inside her.

"Daniel Travis borrowed a considerable sum of money from me," the man explained. Cautiously, he turned to face her and bent his knees a little, as though he was considering whether or not he should obey her. "Dan gave me his house key and insisted I stay here."

"Your name?" she asked, not taking her eyes from the gunsight.

"Wade Reilly."

His name struck a familiar cord inside her, but she was too inflamed at that moment to associate it with anything important. "What did Danny need the money for?" she questioned, keeping the rifle aimed at him.

"Some pressing debts," the man said. When she did not lower her weapon, he added, "I don't know. Perhaps he was threatened by a loan shark."

"Pick up the telephone and dial his number," she instructed.

"I don't possess total recall," he admitted. "The number is in my briefcase."

"It's also on my speed dial," she told him. "The pound key, then number four and press send."

Wade Reilly did as instructed, walking sideways, keeping his eyes on her as he reached for the phone. It seemed an eternity before he spoke again. The few moments gave Nicole time to make some sense out of what she'd just been told.

Two weeks earlier, Danny had called, begging that she send him an enormous amount of money. She adored her brother, but his extravagant lifestyle and his gambling had caused more than one storm in their relationship. She had refused, not only because she felt it was time he learned a lesson, but also because the amount he mentioned was out of her reach. If she sold all of her stocks or cashed in her bonds or mortgaged her half of their property, she could have covered it, but what would that have accomplished? Danny would just end up deeper in debt afterward, perhaps mortgaging his share of their home, and leave her with his monthly payments. She had enabled his reckless lifestyle enough.

If Wade Reilly, standing nearly naked in front of her, actually loaned Danny the amount her brother had requested, they would be in his debt for years. Not that Danny would care. He'd already sent Wade to recover his investment. No doubt Danny expected Nicole to pay Wade off.

Besides, how was Nicole to know whether or not Mr. Reilly even knew Danny? He could have learned her brother's name from the stenciled lettering on their mailbox.

Nicole had just come from Coos Bay Hospital where a life-long neighbor, Matt Hemsley, fought for his life after being assaulted by burglars three days ago. Matt was still in pretty bad shape. Yesterday, the police had visited her home (and the only other house about a mile south of the Hemsleys), advising her to be particularly careful. It was then that Nicole had loaded the rifle above the mantle, just in case.

There had been a rash of burglaries in and around Bandon-by-the-Sea during the past few months. No one would blame Nicole for shooting an intruder in her own home.

"Dan!" Wade barked into the telephone, interrupting Nicole's thoughts. "What did you have in mind, sending me into the home of a lunatic?"

He's probably right, she thought wearily, lowering the rifle to her waist. *I am crazy for putting up with Danny's foolishness in the first place*.

"Will you please try to reason with her?" Wade demanded. "I've tried and nearly had my head blown off for my effort." He listened a moment longer, then held out the receiver to Nicole. "Would-you-kindly-put-the-gun-down?" he asked in clipped tones.

Nicole shrugged grudgingly, but pointed the barrel toward the floor and clicked the safety catch into place, then rested the rifle butt against her hip, the barrel now facing the ceiling at a forty-degree angle from her shoulder. Taking the telephone from Wade with her free hand, she placed the receiver against her ear. "Yes," she sighed.

"Nicole! What's going on out there?" came her brother's familiar voice. His tone was deliberately carefree.

"You tell me," she responded dryly.

"Come on, Nicole. Be reasonable. I had a lot at stake here. Borrowing from Wade was a lifesaver."

"How much?" she asked.

"Now, Nicole, don't blow this up into something tragic."

"How much?" she demanded, this time her voice was crisp and calculating.

Danny mentioned a sum in the six-digit area and her temper skyrocketed.

"That's more than you wanted two weeks ago!" she yelled, thinking how long – all her life – she would be financially obligated to the stranger who stood before her dressed in nothing more than a maroon towel and a few stray drops of water.

"You don't know what I was up against, Sis," Danny explained. "My entire career – No, my entire life, depended on that money. What else could I do?"

"You could have gone to the police," she said, a feeling of dread seeping into her body until she literally ached with it.

"And ruin my only chance for a prosperous future? Nicole, be reasonable. I've only got nine credit hours left before I get my master's degree."

"You've had fourteen credit hours to accumulate in the past three years, Danny. You've only earned five," she added sarcastically. "At this rate, you'll be able to qualify for your master's in another six years." Hooking the receiver against her shoulder, she picked up the telephone and walked over to the mantle.

"Give me a break, Sis," he moaned. "I don't have your talent for whizzing through classes. Be nice to Wade, will you? He saved my life, you know." Then, he added, "Something my own sister was unwilling to do for me."

"Don't even! That guilt-trip stuff will no longer work on me, Danny!" she snapped. "I want you home by tomorrow night. If you're not here by the time I get off work, I'll press charges against you for stealing Mama's jewelry."

"You wouldn't dare!" he challenged, but she also heard the surprise in his voice. Apparently, Danny thought she didn't know it was missing.

"I found it at the pawn shop where you sold it, Danny. It cost me fifteen hundred dollars to buy it back. Fortunately, I also got your signature from the broker's receipt book and the store video showing you as the one who pawned it."

"That jewelry was as much mine as yours!" he insisted.

"No." Nicole shook her head, remembering the specific bequests in her father's will: Danny got Dad's truck, tools and equipment; Nicole got Mama's jewelry and household goods. Refusing to argue the point, she said, "You stole the jewelry. If you're not here by six o'clock tomorrow night, I'll press charges against you."

"You wouldn't!" he dared her.

Wearily, Nicole placed the rifle in its rack above the mantle, then dropped into a nearby overstuffed chair. "Don't tempt me, Danny. Tomorrow night!" She hung up the phone and nodded to Wade. "Make yourself at home," she said bitterly, waving him away with a flick of her hand.

Wade turned and hurried down the hall where he slipped into Danny's bedroom and closed the door. The telephone rang noisily beside her. Nicole knew it was Danny before she even answered it.

"Nicole, don't hang up on me," came Danny's rushed voice as she cradled the receiver to her ear. "You have to understand how desperate I was. Wade literally saved my life."

"Yes," she sighed, "but I wonder if it was worth the effort."

When her brother failed to respond immediately to her caustic remark, she said, "Danny, I've reached my limit with you. I've hauled you out of enough battles to earn the Medal of Honor."

"I'll send you one special delivery, Sis," he persuaded, his voice softening.

"You'll deliver one tomorrow night," she reminded.

"Right," said Danny. "I'll bring you flowers, too. You know I can't survive without you, Nicole. You've always been the level-headed one. Will you forgive me one more time?"

When she was silent, he said, "It's been well over a year since I took Mama's jewelry. You forgave me long ago, Sis, because this is the first time you've even mentioned it."

"No, I didn't forgive you," she said. "I've been waiting for the right moment to force the issue. Guess this is it."

Unfortunately, Nicole's heartstrings tugged in a contrary way to her mind-set. Could she ever really turn her brother in for taking their mother's jewelry? If she could, why hadn't she done so last year when she finally located it in a North Bend pawn shop?

Nicole leaned her head back and stared at the ceiling, draping a levi-clad leg over the arm of the chair. Her mind raced with the recollection that she'd just scared an innocent man out of several years of his life by shooting over his head with her rifle. Level-headed? She almost laughed. After what just happened, Wade Reilly would never believe her capable of anything short of violence.

"Did you sign a contract with Mr. Reilly?" she asked her brother.

The moment's hesitation he gave answered her question even before Danny uttered a re-sounding, "Yes."

"And the terms of the agreement?"

"I sold my stocks to him outright." When he hesitated, Nicole knew what would follow. "Also my share of the real estate. Although I retained the option to repay the debt on the property within three years," he added, as though that would give her some encouragement.

Intuitively, Nicole knew that Danny would never repay Mr. Reilly. If Nicole wanted to continue living in her grandfather's house she would have to pay the real estate debt for Danny, but not without extracting a certain amount of revenge from her brother.

Nicole swallowed the lump that had risen in her throat. "I'll see you tomorrow night, Danny." Before he could say anything more, she added, "Make sure you bring your copy of the contract. I don't trust your Mr. Reilly. Not one bit!"

With this request, she placed the receiver back into its cradle and dropped the telephone to the floor. A string of nasty words suitable for shrieking at Danny's picture on the wall came to mind, but her mouth could not form them. She wanted to vent, to explode in an outburst of angry tears. But no! Crying would not help her, and would probably irritate her new "guest." The only avenue left open to her was to sell her own stocks and bonds, and purchase the real estate back from Mr. Wade Reilly.

Chapter Two

Wearily, Nicole stood and wandered into the kitchen where she put away the groceries, then slumped onto a chrome chair. With her head pounding, she placed her forehead against the cool table top and folded her arms above her head, resting them on the table also.

If only Dad were here! she agonized. Immediately, she heard her father's voice from deep within her heart responding to her silent plea. *"And just where do you think I am, anyway?"* A smile formed on Nicole's lips as she brushed the thought away. *I'm only imagining it. Dad's gone.* Again, her father's words brushed against her heart. *I'm right here, Niki. I'm watching over you and Danny.* His use of the nickname he called Nicole made goose bumps form on her arms and a shiver ran up and down her spine. "Dad, are you there?" she whispered. In answer to her question, silent reality settled upon her and she pushed the strange impressions away. It wasn't the first time she'd thought her father was watching over her, but she had no proof whether it was real or imagined.

Her father was the only one who could control Danny. So far, Nicole had failed entirely. Despite all her encouragement and assistance, her brother was little more than a profligate gambler, a playboy, unable to settle down to anyone or anything.

Nicole Travis, now twenty-nine, was the one who managed the household, made the repairs, paid the utilities, fixed the leaky faucets and replaced the peeling paint and worn shingles. She lifted her head and glanced around the kitchen. A surge of pride welled up within her. The tiled counters and polished oak cupboards would have made her father proud. With the help of her neighbors, the Hemsleys, and Charlie Hackett, her fiancé, they had created quite a few miracles with the old house. Re-roofing was the worst project she had taken on, but now it was finished along with the new carpeting, screens and storm windows. And all of it paid for out of Nicole's hard-earned income. She had just reached the point where she could throw herself into her doctorate work at the Marine Science Institute in

Charleston, Oregon, without worrying continually about the endless list of projects necessary to repair and restore her childhood home.

Closing her eyes and settling her head back upon her folded arms across the kitchen table, Nicole pictured her beloved father from her keen memories of him. Owen Daniel Travis had worked as a logger and tree planter with a local logging company before his untimely death five years ago. His wisdom and foresight had proved substantially beneficial for his daughter and son. With life insurance money he'd left to them, they had been able to pay off the mortgage on their grandfather's Cape Cod style house and had enough money left over for college tuition and a few wise investments. However, the money had never compensated for the loss of her father, who had filled Nicole's youth with fishing trips, deer and bear hunts, and numberless hikes through lush rain forests. She treasured memories that could never be replaced by financial gain.

Her mother passed away before Nicole was nine. Nicole had survived the male influence dominant in her family, which included Grandpa Travis, her father, Owen Daniel, and her brother, Danny. Grandpa Travis died two years after Nicole's mother, when Nicole was eleven years old, leaving Owen to raise Nicole and Danny by himself.

Nicole often thought of her mother, and studied the family photographs of her, particularly a large portrait in the living room above the roll-top desk. During the past twenty years, she worried about the masculine environment that had surrounded her teen years. *Tough as a mama bear, tender as an angel's hair,* her father used to say of her. She knew this saying was true, for she had seen both sides of her character . . . especially with her soft spot for Danny. For years she had worried if she would ever be womanly enough for a man to take an interest in her. Had she inherited enough of her mama's charm to find maternal skills inside when she would need them? Nicole believed her dad knew all along that she could meet any challenge tossed at her. Owen Travis often referred to Nicole as "little mother" because she had taken over the raising of her brother, Danny, two years younger than herself. Occasionally, her dad reminded her that Danny was not her child.

Thinking of Danny now, Nicole realized she had never stopped mothering him. Perhaps she was the root from which his problems stemmed. He had never been forced to grow up, for Nicole was always available to bail him out of any difficulty. But not this time, she vowed. She had nothing left to give him. The best she could do for him at this point was to sell her stocks, purchase back Danny's portion of the real estate, and become the sole owner of her grandfather's house and the two hundred acres surrounding it. At least Danny would have nothing left that they owned together with which to torment her. He would have to suffer the consequences of his own actions because he had sold his stocks and bonds to Wade Reilly, as well as his share of the real estate. If Nicole bought Danny's share of the property away from him, Danny would have only himself to lean upon. She would not, could not, allow him to take her down with him. Not again!

"Asleep?" came a startling male voice, intruding into her private thoughts.

Nicole opened her eyes and stared up at Wade Reilly. He towered above her on the other side of the kitchen table. His broad shoulders appeared more threatening when covered by a heavy cotton sweater, indigo with a silver and black striping pattern. Beneath the sweater he wore another shirt with an unusual plaid design made of blue and gray flannel. Muscled legs were covered by gray slacks that rested low on his hips, emphasizing the narrowness of his waist. The color of his sweater only made his sky-blue eyes more startling. His eyes were framed by thick, ebony lashes that curled at the tips. Full lips formed a perfect mouth above a squarish chin. His hair was a dark, coffee brown with lots of sheen to it.

"I – " she stammered. "I'm sorry I frightened you."

"Sorry?" he questioned, his tone rising in volume to match his temper. "Sorry is when a child breaks a vase or soils a tablecloth! A bent knee and a fervent plea for mercy would be more appropriate!"

"For what?" she demanded, her temper matching his. "Missing you?"

"By the grace of God," he replied soberly.

Nicole stood up, hoping to gain some leverage, but his height made her seem minuscule in comparison. "That bullet was not meant to hit you," she hissed. "The bullet struck exactly where aimed."

"High and to the right," he reminded with sarcasm. "You expect me to believe you missed intentionally?"

"Come with me!" she snapped, walking past him toward the living room. She was jerked forcefully back when he wrapped strong fingers around her arm.

"Tell me," he said, his lips curling in a sneer. "Is it your habit to welcome Dan home with such warmth and enthusiasm?"

"I don't know what you mean. I thought you were a burglar."

"Just coming out of the shower?" he challenged scornfully, his grip loosening.

"There have been several break-ins around here." She shrugged her arm away from him. "The police were here just yesterday warning me to be cautious. You parked your car around back, like you were trying to hide it. And it looks nothing like Danny's truck or a rental. What else was I supposed to think?"

"That your husband bought a new Lexus?" he questioned.

"A Lexus?" Her voice squeaked.

"How many burglars do you think drive around in a Lexus?"

"It could have been stolen," she argued.

"More likely, you were so angry with your husband for buying a new car that you were ready to shoot him," he suggested with a dark, mocking scowl.

"What makes you think Danny and I are married?" she asked, her eyes widening in disbelief.

"Come now! You are living in *his* house. You share the same last name. You must think me terribly gullible."

"Try dense," she accused.

Ignoring her jibe, Wade pointed accusingly at her, and said, "No wonder Dan prefers to remain in Denver. He's married to a regular shrew."

"Wrong," she announced dryly. "Danny's never been married. And I don't love him THAT much! He's my brother."

Wade dropped his hand quickly and forced a look of surprise upon his face. He allowed a derisive smile to form around his mouth. "Insanity must run in the family."

Nicole's patience failed completely with his remark. "You want insanity?" she questioned. "I'll show you what insanity really is!" She ground the heel of her boot against the floor and turned sharply. When he hesitated, she gave him a challenging smile, "Unless, of course, you're a coward."

Wade followed immediately and she preceded him into the living room. In the far corner stood a handsome antique trophy case, bedecked with numerous trophies, all with sharp-shooter figures. Each one bore the name Nicole Travis. While he carefully inspected each one of them, Nicole said, "You were angry that I wouldn't allow you an explanation, yet you deny me the same privilege. Perhaps the only reason why I could be accused of insanity is because I spared you."

"Impressive," he muttered. The full realization of her marksmanship had its impact. He had his work cut out for him, Wade decided. *This is going to take more wit and persuasion than I originally thought.* If Nicole Travis even suspected the true reason for his presence in her home, she wouldn't hesitate to demonstrate her skill with firearms . . . straight through his heart. He had thought this would be an easy assignment. Now, he would have to re-evaluate.

Nicole continued her conversation. "Bandon has had seven robberies in as many weeks. One of my dearest friends was burglarized three days ago, and he's still in the hospital. He had come home earlier than expected, surprising the burglars, and was beaten cruelly in return. I've just come from visiting him at the hospital. On the way home, I resolved that no one would get the opportunity to do to me what they did to my friend. So you can imagine how I felt when I found a naked man streaking toward my brother's bedroom."

Wade turned around, keeping his expression fearful, hoping he looked relieved that she had spared him. "Little wonder you fired your rifle at me," he said. "However, I doubt a burglar would bother to take a shower before robbing your house."

"I had only two conclusions I could draw when I first saw you walking up the hall in nothing but a bath towel," she asserted. "You were either Matt Hemsley's assailant or a rapist. Perhaps both."

"I am neither," he reassured her. "And rapists do not usually bathe first. It was a long drive from Denver. I hadn't stopped to rest, but drove straight through. It's a good twenty-four hours road-time. Your brother will be lucky to make your deadline tomorrow night."

"Danny can make it in twenty," she insisted, "if he doesn't get picked up for speeding. But he'll probably take the midnight flight and rent a car in North Bend. That's what he usually does."

"Why did you spare me?" he asked, changing the subject abruptly, and stepping closer, almost touching her.

She looked up at him, apparently mulling his question around in her mind. Wade used her hesitation to study her thoughtfully. The fire in her light brown eyes softened, and he could feel the innocence in her that belied the feistiness of character he had seen. He wanted to put his arms around her, to comfort her. The silkiness of her chestnut brown hair framing her strikingly beautiful oval face, the slight moisture in her eyes, the provocative point of indecision on her lips made him aware of the desire and promise she radiated as a woman. Her nearness seemed to create an aura of intimacy between them that

he could physically feel. Wade resolved to protect her even more fiercely, regardless of the
personal cost to himself.

"Well?" he finally asked. "I'm waiting."

"I – " she stammered. Then she gave him a
mischievous grin. "I don't make it a habit to shoot
undressed game."

To this remark, his mouth curved up at the
corners in a disarming smile, accenting dimples
on both sides of his face.

"Are you hungry?" she asked quickly, hoping to establish a silent truce between them.

Her eyes were drawn to his, and she worried that he would see the tumult of emotion puls-
ing through her at his almost intimate contact.
Her face burned and she felt as though he had
touched her in a personal way that made her
shiver with delight. Could he possibly know what
was going on inside her petite body as she stared
up at him in complete wonder?

Other questions troubled her. Why should
she feel this way when she was already engaged
to a perfectly awesome man? Why, in the three
months of her engagement, had she not felt like
this when her fiancé, Charlie Hackett, looked at
her? Nicole felt positively naked, regardless that
she was wearing jeans and a form fitting shirt
with a sweetheart neckline. As she looked up at

his face, their eyes locked. His eyes were so blue they reminded her of peaceful days she had spent at sea this past summer, of the brilliant sky overhead and the still, calm water. For some inexplicable reason, her breathing stopped momentarily and she felt giddy and light-headed. Although Wade was handsome, there was something else about him, something indefinable that made her heart tremble with a new and exciting emotion. Fearing he would notice, she broke the spell by glancing down at the floor. Clearing her throat, Nicole asked again, "Are you hungry? I've not eaten since noon. I could fix something for both of us."

"I stopped at a little restaurant in the old section of Bandon along the waterfront. I had a hamburger big enough to cover a dinner plate."

"The Minute Café," she stated, realizing at once where he'd gone for supper. "They serve delicious food."

"Yes, but this is Oregon, not Texas. Are all their sandwiches that enormous?"

Nicole grinned and nodded. "I guess that's what makes them one of the town favorites."

"Your brother mentioned the ocean is not far from here. I believe he said a path leads from your property right onto the beach. Perhaps you could show it to me in the morning?"

"If you walk behind the garden out back, you won't miss it. I have to leave by 6:30 A. M."

"Every morning?" he asked, arching an eyebrow.

"Nearly," she agreed, walking back into the kitchen. She felt a faint dizziness when she realized he had followed her.

Opening the refrigerator, Nicole took out a bowl of salad greens and a tomato. Using a cutting board and a tomato knife, she diced the tomato into half-inch cubes. The entire time she worked in the kitchen Wade watched her. He leaned against the doorframe that led into the hall and made a careful study of her, from the leather boots she wore, and upward. Her usual working attire was denim pants and a form-fitting blouse, comfortable and convenient for her line of work. Tonight she could feel his eyes upon her and suddenly she was conscious of her legs, hugged by the denim fabric, and her lean hips. Her blouse seemed totally inadequate under his scrutiny. Shoulder-length chestnut hair cascaded around her face and across her shoulders in a damp flurry of curls, a constant reminder of the high humidity level along the Oregon Coast.

When her salad was ready, she topped it with a hard-boiled egg and homemade French dressing. Then, Nicole placed her supper on the table and sat down to eat.

Wade sat across from her. He watched, but remained silent as she munched on her salad. "You make me feel self-conscious," she said between mouthfuls.

"Serves you right," he agreed. "How do you think I felt earlier? A woman I was not expecting, barging in on me with a rifle in hand. And me with nothing on but a bath towel."

Nicole blushed. She hadn't been as concerned with how he was dressed when she first accosted him, she was more concerned that he was there at all. Refusing to respond to his question, she said, "Danny's bedding is clean. I make it a point to change it immediately when he leaves. I never know but what he'll be back before nightfall."

"Since you're an early riser, don't bother to wake me. I plan to sleep late tomorrow morning. You won't mind if I turn in early?" he asked.

"I doubt I'll be home until after Danny gets here tomorrow night," she responded. "And I lock my bedroom door, in case you were wondering."

"So do I," he admitted, but she heard the hint of a challenge in his tone.

Wade stood and walked down the hall. Nicole listened to the bedroom door click shut before returning to her salad.

Later that night, just before falling asleep in her locked bedroom, a thought crept into Nicole's mind that made her cheeks burn. The moment by the corner shelf stayed with her a long time. It seemed as though she and Wade had reached out and touched one another in an intimate, almost tangible way. The exciting current of attraction between them was more powerful than anything she'd ever felt. It wasn't until Nicole realized she was probably the only one who experienced this strange and wonderful sensation that she closed her mind to it.

Depression crept over her like a dark cloak. Wade had given no indication that he was affected whatsoever by her. Only the reverse was true.

Chapter Three

Nicole rolled over and pushed the button down on the alarm. With her other hand, she rubbed her tight stomach, wondering why she felt so queasy. She would have to hurry this morning. Her employer, Philip Thompson, would be at the institute early, cleaning and making final preparations for the arrival of Dr. Reilly.

"Dr. E. W. Reilly!" she mouthed aloud as she sat straight up in bed. *Eugene Wade Reilly! He's the one Dr. Thompson is expecting!* Dr. E. W. Reilly wasn't just a marine biologist and oceanographer. Nicole's mind buzzed with sudden recollection. Wade Reilly was the Jacques Cousteau of her employer's world!

Feeling suddenly very ill, a wave of nausea assailed her and she moaned, jumped out of bed and raced to the bathroom where she lost what little fluid remained in her stomach from last night.

Afterward, she washed her face and reached for a hand towel. Wiping all traces of moisture from her lips, she looked into the mirror to see Wade Reilly's derisive frown reflected there.

Slowly, Nicole turned around to face him, wondering why he was up so early. Realizing she had probably awoken him, she moaned.

"Do you always start your mornings this violently?" he questioned. "Or is this a case of nine-month syndrome?"

His words stung at the back of her eyes. "None of your business!" she lashed out, pushing him out of the bathroom and slamming the door in his face. Suppressing the temptation to belittle herself further in his eyes by swearing at him, she stared at her reflection without seeing the pallid complexion or dark shadows beneath her brown eyes.

Nicole heard a knock on the bathroom door. "My sister was pregnant once," Wade called through the closed door when she refused to answer. "She used to eat dry toast and Seven-Up every morning. Would you like some?"

Nicole refused to answer. She took a quick shower, brushed her teeth, restored some color to her cheeks and studied the hint of amber in her dark brown eyes in the mirror. *Terrific!* She thought miserably. *I've completely alienated the one man Dr. Thompson expected me to befriend.*

The instructions from her employer yesterday were explicit: "Come in early, Miss Travis. We want to impress Dr. Reilly. It would benefit the Marine Institute financially and intellectually if he were to make our area his home. Think of the prestige, just associating his name with ours! Not to mention the government grants we could procure. Nothing must run amiss with Dr. Reilly in our presence. Nothing!"

Nicole never really thought of Dr. Reilly as having a first given name. She always thought of him as Dr. Reilly, not Wade. He was internationally known for his research on red tides. Because of his tireless pursuit, many areas were now identified long before the toxins could build up in shellfish and crustaceans. Several college textbooks had been written by Dr. Reilly, not to mention his best-seller non-fiction titles. Her own knowledge could be placed on a penny compared to his wealth of marine science information and experience. Somehow, she hadn't expected him to be so handsome.

According to Dr. Thompson, Wade trained under descendants of Jacques Cousteau, but had accomplished a great deal in his own right. Having met Wade Reilly, Nicole did not share Dr.

Thompson's enthusiasm. The man she met last night was hot-tempered, arrogant and unforgiving.

For one brief moment she recalled the sensation of pleasure that excited her the previous night when their eyes locked and she had fantasized about Wade reaching out to her in a physical, intimate embrace. The memory would be etched upon her soul forever. She shivered and wished it had all really happened: his body touching hers, her mouth seeking his warmth, his lips exploring her curves.

Stop it! she demanded. *Wade experienced none of your senseless delusions. He thinks you're a lunatic, nothing short of completely insane.*

Besides, she reminded herself, she had to think about Charlie. She'd promised to marry Charlie in December. They'd been making preparations for three months. Was she going to throw it all away just because another man had looked at her with a little interest?

Charlie Hackett was a successful fisherman, both sport and commercial, with two fishing trawlers and a charter service craft that were capable of catering to the most discerning clientele. When they met less than a year ago, it had seemed the impossible dream. They dated frequently and when he asked her to marry him, she had given him an emphatic yes. Charlie was handsome with his sandy blonde hair and gray-green eyes, plus a youthful face despite his forty years. He had been married once before, but his wife left him, apparently for another man.

It took Nicole several months to convince Charlie she was not the straying type. Only here she was, staring at herself in the mirror and wishing she had spent the night in Wade Reilly's bed, instead of her own!

Nicole sighed wistfully, forcing thoughts of Wade aside. Charlie was everything a woman could want in a man. Thoughtful. Kind and generous. Financially stable. He made her feel special no matter what she did. He was always careful to control his temper in front of her, although she had heard rumors that he could fight if the need arose. She had never seen a mean streak in him, as a few of the townsmen suggested to her. He'd never once argued nor raised his voice to her. He always gave in, letting her make the decisions. What more could she want in a future husband?

Styling her hair with a curling iron, she watched as the shadow of her arm fell across her face. Just because she never felt the same exhilarating dizziness with Charlie that she'd experienced last night with Wade didn't mean she couldn't feel that way sometime with Charlie. As soon as they were married, and he helped her overcome her timidity where intimacy was concerned, she would be caught up in the passion of lovemaking, wouldn't she?

The shadow on her face remained across her memories, reminding her of a time thirteen years ago when she went on her first date. She had been an ecstatic, sixteen-year-old on her first date without a chaperone. What a disaster! It was a good thing Danny, always protective of his older sister, had followed her that night. Otherwise . . . Nicole shuddered. How was she to know a man could be so violent? *Sweet sixteen and never been kissed*, her father used to say. Even he had no idea what transpired that awful June evening, nor why Danny came home looking as though he'd been mauled by a bear. Actually, if Danny hadn't won the battle, she would have looked just as bad. Perhaps worse. Shivering, Nicole brushed such thoughts from her mind as swiftly as she brushed the curls of her tawny brown hair.

Finally satisfied she looked presentable, Nicole peeked around the bathroom door. Wade was nowhere in sight, so she made a quick dash for her bedroom where she dressed casually in her leather boots, a pair of tan jeans and a feminine, cream-taffeta western blouse with dark brown stitching. A silky cream ribbon tied in her hair gave her the added touch of femininity she wanted.

Glancing at her watch, Nicole realized she would not have time for breakfast. As unsettled as her stomach still felt, food would only complicate matters.

Nicole headed for the kitchen to retrieve her handbag and ran straight into Wade, who was coming around the corner with a glass of milk and a plate of toast.

"My blouse!" she moaned as the white liquid drained down the front of her. "Oh, Pickles! Now look what you've done!"

"Pickles?" he asked, unable to suppress a smile.

"It's less offensive than something else I could have said," she retorted. "Or would you have preferred *Oh* – "

"Pickles will do," he grinned. "My sister preferred pickles, too. I'm sorry about the milk, though."

She tugged at the wet fabric, pulling it away from her skin.

"May I get you a towel?" he asked, stepping closer to her than the circumstances required. "Or help you out of that wet blouse?" He arched his eyebrows up and down twice and grinned mischievously.

Just standing this close to him was enough to frazzle Nicole's nerves, without him trying to sop up the milk with a towel while making evocative remarks. The milk could have boiled on her skin beneath the blouse. She wasn't certain that he couldn't see steam rising up from her heated chest.

"Listen!" she snapped, unable to quell half the emotions running rampant within her. "I got along just fine before you showed up! I'm perfectly capable of removing my own clothing, and handling a mild case of the flu!"

"Or whatever," he taunted.

"Or whatever!" she challenged, unwilling to correct him. "Which, as I've said already this morning, is none of your business!"

"I suppose that means you don't want the toast?" Wade gave her a weak smile.

"I don't want anything from you but to get you out of my house!" she insisted.

"Our house," he corrected.

"Just as soon as Danny gets here and I have a chance to peruse your contract, to see if it's even legal – "

"It is legal," he interrupted.

"Then I'll arrange the sale of my stocks and bonds and pay off Danny's debt on the house. Believe me, it will soon become *my* house entirely!"

"What makes you think I'll accept your money? My agreement is with your brother, not you. Quite frankly, I hope he can't redeem the contract on the real estate. I wouldn't mind staying here, perhaps buying out *your* share." His eyebrow arched, indicating the seriousness of his intentions.

"Over my dead body!" Nicole hissed.

"I doubt that," Wade said, baiting her. "I don't make it a habit to shoot game in any form, dressed or undressed."

Nicole shook her dark curls and turned around, went back into her bedroom and grabbed another blouse from the closet. Walking back toward the bathroom, she glanced at her watch. It was twenty minutes to seven. She should have left ten minutes ago.

To her dismay, Wade had already entered the bathroom and locked the door. "Wade?" she said, knocking on the door. "How long will you be? I have to go to work, you know."

The door was jerked open and he stared angrily down at her. "You are the most bothersome, irritating creature I have ever had the displeasure to meet!" he remarked, a whisper of tension in his voice.

Nicole couldn't decide if he was teasing or serious. "And who do you think you are?" she retorted. "Mr. Wonderful?"

Wade did not reply, but stepped aside so she could enter. "It's all yours, Nicole."

"You can call me Miss Travis," she snapped, losing patience with him entirely.

"I like Nicole," he said, ignoring her angry demand. "The name, that is."

It was a qualification that made her stomach retch for the second time that morning. Rushing past him, she slammed the door and bent over in agony. After a few moments, she realized it was a false alarm. Willing her temper to a semblance of control was no easy task, but she finally succeeded and cleaned up her sticky skin, then redressed in a pale yellow blouse with green accents that today made her face seem sallow.

Nicole, finally ready to leave, had her hand on the front doorknob when Wade called out, "Nicole, wait." She glared reprovingly at him when he appeared under the archway. "What hours do you work?" he asked.

"From seven to five-thirty, four days a week."

"What are your days off?"

"Friday, Saturday and Sunday. Why?"

"We get along so splendidly," he scoffed, "I thought I'd try to make myself scarce when you're home, and vice versa while I'm here. I will be working in Charleston, but I'm not certain of my schedule. At the rate our friendship is

progressing, we need an amiable agreement between us so we can spend less time together."
Wade gave her a crooked grin that made her
heart tremble.

"Like friendship with you is ever going to
happen in my lifetime!" she chided.

Ignoring her comment, he said, "Perhaps by
evening we can come to some mutual terms for
use of the bathroom and the kitchen."

He apparently had no idea that Nicole
worked at the Marine Institute in Charleston,
which was exactly where he was headed later
in the day. Nicole took a moment to contemplate
a healthy retort, and noticed his chest was bare
beneath the long "V" of his blue bathrobe. Nicole
found her eyes drawn to the thin scattering of
hair upon his chest. For the second time in her
life, she felt as though he was undressing her
with his eyes. Heedlessly, she reciprocated, recalling with exact clarity how he looked partially
nude, an advantage he did not have over her.
Wade was well-muscled, his skin bronzed by the
summer sun, and tall, a fact she was reminded
of by having to tilt her chin up to look at his face.

A gnawing sensation filled her lower stomach and she placed a hand over it, wondering if
he knew what he could do to her with a casual
glance up and down her well-clothed body. Im-

mediately, a frown crossed over his face, as though he were angry with her. Perhaps looking at him in the same hungry way he had studied her was out of bounds.

Turning around, Nicole hurried out to the car.

After starting her yellow Mini Cooper, Nicole rolled down the driver's side window, put the car in gear and headed west onto Beach Loop Drive, past the Blue Jay Campground, then north toward Bandon. Tall Douglas pines loomed up on her right while salt brush stubbled the sand to her left. Within a few minutes, she was well past Face Rock View Point and the Garden of the Gods, a group of rock formations along the Pacific Coast. When she finally reached Ocean Drive, she turned left at Edison and east again along First Street to the Boat Basin. Although this was the long way around, Coast Highway 101 would have been much faster, she faithfully drove these back roads every day when she went to work. Something about the drive set her mind at ease. Perhaps the fact that she had covered every inch of coastline numerous times with her father in the days of her youth and it comforted her. This route drew her back to the southwest part of Bandon.

The pull of the ocean was like a wild and uncontrollable force within her. Listening to the pounding of monstrous waves as they relentlessly devoured the sandy beaches, making this part of the world an endless cycle of change somehow released the tensions of her hectic world.

Crashing seawater was a soothing balm to Nicole, sometimes so much so she wondered why she had not been born a mermaid. If she had, she certainly would not be facing a multi-dimensional problem like Wade Reilly.

Chapter Four

As Nicole drove through the Boat Basin, she could see Charlie Hackett's fleet of fishing boats fastened to their moorings, resting like ducks upon the water. She was disappointed not to see her fiancé aboard any of them, although his brothers, Bo and Devin, were both stretched out in hammocks supported by the rigging aboard two of the fishing vessels, no doubt hung over from drinking too much the night before. Why Charlie put up with their nonsense, Nicole still did not understand. Except that Charlie had a soft spot for them, much like the tenderness she had for Danny.

"Nicole!" came a booming voice as she started to pass by the Arcade Tavern.

Taking her eyes from the road, Nicole noticed Charlie standing between the tavern and the feed store. She pulled the Cooper over and stopped next to the boardwalk.

Charlie walked to her car and bent over. "Everything okay, Babe?" he asked, his burly hand upon the driver's side window well.

"Fine, Charlie. I got a late start this morning."

He poked his head through the window space and kissed her cheek. "Mmm," he mused. "You're trembling. Sure you're okay?"

"I'm all right. A touch of flu, I think. But today's an important day at the MIC, so I couldn't call in sick."

"Nothing else wrong, is there, Babe?" he asked, his voice betraying a moment of doubt.

"Everything is fine!" she exclaimed, planting her lips against his cheek. Surely Charlie didn't know anything about Wade staying overnight at her house, did he?

"Did you get home safely last night?" her fiancé asked. Before she could answer, he said, "After what happened to Matt Hemsley, I keep thinking I should start staying at your place."

"Don't worry. I'm ordering a security system today," she responded, giving him a brief smile, more in relief than any other emotion. Charlie was worried about the burglaries in Bandon-by-the-Sea, that's all. She was glad she would not have to tell him anything else just yet.

It would be difficult for Charlie to learn she now shared her house with a man, a stranger in a bath towel she met last night. Charlie didn't have to know about Wade if she could get the matter settled within a couple of days. She would pay Danny's debt off and send Wade packing. Charlie would never understand, and after the torment Charlie's first wife put him through, he certainly didn't need to feel Wade was competition.

"I'm going to be late, Charlie," she said, straightening in her seat. "It's after seven and I was supposed to come in early. I'm sorry."

"We're still going fishing on Saturday, aren't we?"

"Absolutely," she agreed.

"Bye, Nicole. I'll call you." He backed up, giving her room to drive away.

So far so good, she thought to herself. Charlie was no more aware of Wade's presence than Nicole was before she arrived home last night. And with a little luck, Charlie need never know.

Nicole sighed in relief when she turned off the highway onto Seven Devils Road. Just a few more miles and she would only be twelve minutes late. Several sharp turns in the road kept her mind occupied. Although she had traveled Seven Devils hundreds of times during the past three years, she would never adjust to the twisting and winding that brought her to the Marine Institute at Charleston, called MIC by the locals. Sometimes it seemed as though she was driving through a winding tunnel with tall Douglas fir, standing as sentinels on both sides of her little Cooper, reaching toward the sky and blocking out all sunlight.

Within minutes Nicole arrived at the Institute, an old brick building, single level, with white-framed windows and a low roof line. Two newer cinder block buildings stood behind it. She was surprised to see Dr. Thompson, pacing back and forth in the hallway when she opened the back door, his bony hands folded behind a short, wiry body.

"Miss Travis!" he exclaimed immediately, tucking his fists into his white cotton overcoat. "Don't stand around gawking, we have work to do. Dr. Reilly telephoned to say he has arrived in the area. He'll be here in time for lunch. I've taken the liberty of ordering a meal catered by the Pearl, so that the staff can spend the noon hour getting to know him."

"Oh?" Nicole asked, pretending she was unaware of Wade's whereabouts.

"Yes, and we don't have a minute to lose. I've decided we should rotate the crab lamps as you suggested yesterday. That will take most of the morning."

Nicole gave him a knowing frown.

"I know!" he defended crossly. "I should have listened, but my mind wasn't on the crab lamps. After Dr. Reilly's letter arrived last week announcing he would be in our area, I've thought of little else."

"I noticed," she answered meekly. Giving him time to gather loose ends, Nicole stepped into her shared office and slid her purse in the bottom drawer of her desk.

Nancy Cardston, an efficient, elderly secretary was typing at the front desk, her face so wrinkled it was difficult to identify the thin line of her lips, pursed intensely as she focused on the task at hand, her round-rimmed bifocals loosely bridged over her bumpy nose. Noticing Nicole arrive, Nancy gave her a cordial greeting. "Good morning, Miss Travis."

"You don't have to pretend on my account," Nicole whispered. "I know Dr. Thompson's been a bear this morning with his Lordship arriving today."

Nancy frowned and pushed her glasses higher on her nose. "I feel so ashamed," she confessed with a conspiratorial grin. "I actually thought of pushing the good doctor into the shark tank this morning." A big smile wrinkled her aged face even more. "But I'm too young to face a life sentence," she added hastily and winked.

Nicole laughed. Nancy always seemed to lighten the mood at the Institute. They would be hard-pressed to replace her with any equal. Nancy could have retired fifteen years ago, but she claimed she would have nothing to do if she didn't stay working at MIC.

"Could I ask a big favor?" Nicole asked Nancy.

"Anything for you," Nancy answered kindly.

"You just had a home security system installed by Oregon Coast Alarm, right?"

Nancy nodded. "Best investment we ever made. You should– "

"Would you call them," Nicole interrupted, "and ask them to come out to my place and install a new system for me? I want the best they've got, their deluxe package. Several people, including our local sheriff, recommended OCA as the best security server in the area. I've decided it's time to do it."

"I'll call them first thing this morning. You know, Miss Travis, if you install a system and use my name as a referral, I'll get two months free service."

"Make sure they give it to you, then." Nicole gave her a warm smile. "Tell them to come out on Friday morning to install it. I'll be home that day."

Nancy gave her a happy thumbs up, and Nicole went to the pop machine where she put in her quarters and pressed the Seven-Up button. After getting the can of soda, she picked up her white jacket from her locker, then walked down the main hall to Claude Browning's classroom, sipping the bubbly liquid. It felt good going down, but once it reached her stomach, she began to feel queasy again. Perhaps she would dispense with the beverage.

Claude Browning's class would be studying advanced crustacean life forms this week. Seeking his assistance with the lamps would probably be best. The classroom door was open and Claude was at the chalkboard, drawing a detailed crab anatomy.

"Good morning, Miss Travis," he nodded, glancing up from the text in his hand. "What can I do for you?" Claude was always formal when addressing her at the Institute, but without, he often reverted to her given name, Nicole.

"For starters," she said, "let me dump this soda down your sink."

"Easy favors," he teased. "That's the spirit, Miss Travis."

"That's the easy one," she agreed. "The other is to put your class into action today. Dr. Thompson has agreed to my suggestion about the crab lamps."

"Easy twice," he smiled, slapping his book shut and tossing it on his desk. "I was not in the mood for dissecting old *Callinectes Sapidus* today, anyway."

"Thanks," she said. "I didn't think I could face it by myself. Not today."

"You do look a bit peaked," Claude observed. "Virus?"

"Undoubtedly," she agreed.

"I hope you're well enough for the hunt," he said, erasing the chalkboard. "Margo says her brother, Bill, scouted the coast range around the Siuslaw North Fork and found bear tracks everywhere."

"That's seven weeks away," she reminded as she arched an eyebrow and gave him a knowing smile. Claude lived for the bear hunt, even though he never once shot a bear. Nicole changed the subject. "How is Margo?"

"Splendid now that the gazebo has been installed, the one for which she's been begging the past eleven years. But I can't complain. My wife's inside track to bear hunting news is legendary, so she's already repaid the favor." He gave her a conspiratorial wink. "You remember old Brubaker?"

Nicole nodded. "The hermit who always visits our camp. My father developed a friendship with him, you know. Brubaker and Dad used to visit on most of his hunting trips." A vision of the tart-tongued, aged recluse filled her memories as vividly as real life. Brubaker was the most talked about and least seen member of the community in all of Bandon. Legends about Brubaker were retold at every campfire within a forty-mile radius. Yet Nicole had never found Brubaker to be anything more than an old man who wanted to be left alone. Hermit didn't even begin to describe his reclusive habits.

"Brubaker told Margo's brother this summer that he took out a big black bear in the spring that was after his chickens. Says he's seen dozens of bear since then."

"Hmm. Hunting out of season again, is he?" she asked.

They both laughed. Everyone who knew anything about old Brubaker knew that he did as he pleased on his own property. But he was harmless to humans; left them alone and expected them to leave him alone.

"I'm sure Matt will be feeling better long before the hunt," she said. "Do you think his doctor will still let him go? Somehow it wouldn't be the same without Matt along."

"A shame about Matt," Claude echoed her sentiment. "But if I know anything at all about that man, it'll take more than a couple of burglars to keep him from the hunt. He's too ornery to keep down for long."

They were interrupted when a flood of college-age students came charging into the classroom, ready and eager for a new day. It never ceased to amaze Nicole how devoted the students were in their endeavor to master marine biology.

Soon, she was leading Claude Browning's class members into the building that housed the crab project. This large aquarium-room had been her research area for the past two years during which time she had struggled and stretched her mind beyond what she thought she was capable of, but now, the crab project was going much better. She had until the end of November to complete her thesis. Hopefully, her research and written reports would then help Nicole earn her doctorate in marine biology.

Around the double door frames to the cinder block building, etched in the wood, were these words from the poet, John Masefield:

I must go down to the seas again, for the call of the running tide
Is a wild call and a clear call that may not be denied.

It always made Nicole shiver to read it, for she understood the call of the sea. It was more than a force to be reckoned with, her passion for the ocean consumed her time and held her interest incessantly.

When Claude asked Nicole to explain the crab project for his students, she did not hesitate. "It all began in Louisiana when scientists decided they could domesticate blue crabs, producing bigger crabs faster than the commercial crabbers could catch them. The objective of their project was to fool the crabs into thinking a full day had passed by when they alternated light and dark periods of time. Gradually, the time was shortened until the blue crabs were growing as quickly in sixteen hours as they normally grew in twenty-four hours. Our study is similar, except that we are using the much meatier Dungeness crabs and we're using less time which is more scientifically regulated. Right now our crabs are thriving on seven hours daylight and six hours darkness, providing almost thirteen days a week for the crabs to grow. The project is working."

Nicole waited a moment for the clapping to cease, and continued. "Our crabs are feeding as much in one thirteen-hour period as they would have in twenty-four hours, and their growth rate is phenomenal. Today, we will be moving their lamps to represent the sunlight as it changes in the fall from directly overhead as it was in the summer, to ten degrees southward. When winter arrives, we will move the lamps still farther south. The experiment has never been taken to this level before, so it is entirely unprecedented."

"Couldn't this process be automated?" asked one young man in the class.

"With enough funding, certainly," said Nicole. "But until that funding is available to us, this is a manual project. The domestication of the Dungeness crab has not been proven detrimental in any area of our research."

After a fair amount of time in questions and answers, the class began the tedious task of moving the lamps ten degrees to the south. Several times during the discussion, Nicole experienced a momentary dizziness, combined with severe stomach pains, but prayed she would be able to make it through the rest of the day. Luckily, her duties after the luncheon with Dr. Reilly and the staff would be confined mostly to desk work at her computer.

When the lamps were repositioned, Nicole headed toward her shared office where she planned to chart the morning's events in her log book and spend a few moments dictating the progress of the experiment into a hand-held recorder. The morning passed all too quickly. Nicole was dismayed to find herself dreading the arrival of Dr. E. Wade Reilly.

How would Wade react to their working together since that very morning he had insisted they try to avoid one another? Would he be disappointed to learn that Nicole was also a marine biologist? Judging from his texts, which she thumbed through and put back on an office shelf, Wade was a perfectionist, a professional who did not allow for human error nor outdated equipment. Perhaps the combination of a fifty-year-old aquarium and even older lighting systems, and Nicole herself, would prove more trial than Wade could endure. The Institute might be laughed right out of commission by Dr. Wade Reilly.

If so, Nicole would have only herself to blame. She could have spent some of her own money on the crab lab project. Instead, she had used it to restore and repair her house . . . a

house she neither owned completely, nor dis-
owned . . . a house she shared with Wade Reilly.

Nicole had applied for every single grant
she could find to fund the crab lab, and so far
she'd been successful. Of course, Wade Reilly's
scientific insight would, perhaps, be set on something a bit more profitable. He would undoubtedly be highly amused at her attempt to capture the crab market. And though her motives
were strictly honorable, perhaps her methods
would be beneath his standards. Surely he would
soon realize that all she wanted was a way to
fill the world's need for large amounts of
crabmeat in less time for less money. It was
never a get-rich-quick scheme, just a simple
way to help feed hungry people. Would Wade
berate her for the attempt?

Truthfully, if the experiment showed promise, she had considered pitching the idea to some
budding young student living near the Alaskan
King Crab industry as a possible study project.

Why Nicole was so concerned over how
Wade would react she did not understand. When
she considered the project rationally, she realized that Wade's opinion would not alter the success of what she had accomplished so far. Why
was she plaguing herself with too many concerns
about Wade's opinion, anyway? Why was it so

important to her that Wade was pleased with the crab project? What difference would it make if he hated the whole idea?

Unable to answer any of the doubts troubling her, Nicole reached her shared office to find Charlie Hackett waiting for her. Since her fiancé had never stepped foot inside the Institute before today, he caught her completely off guard.

She was unaware that the expression of surprise on her face gave Charlie the impression that she was guilty without ever being charged with a crime.

Nicole studied her fiancé with astute precision. He was not only pale, but his green eyes were almost gray with emotion. Was he angry? She could not decide. "What is it?" she asked, concern for Charlie's unexpected presence in her office seemed to tighten an invisible band around her chest.

"Can you get away for lunch, Babe?" he asked, sweat breaking out on his forehead. He wiped it away with a handkerchief from his jeans' pocket and stood up.

"I – " she stammered, about to finish the sentence with *can't*. She should stay long enough to be introduced to Dr. E. Wade Reilly and sit through the Pearl's catered luncheon pushing around food she did not have the stomach for that day. But Charlie's desperate expression changed her mind. "I'd be delighted," she said with a bright smile, wrapping her arms about his waist in an affectionate embrace. "Just give me a minute to clear it with Nancy."

Walking over to the coffee pot where Nancy was pouring a cup, Nicole said, "Something's come up. I'll have to slip away for an hour. Do you think you can control Dr. Thompson when he finds out?"

Nancy coughed, sputtered and spilled coffee on the floor. "And miss the luncheon?" she gasped.

Nicole nodded, but gave her a grimace, as well.

Inhaling sharply, Nancy turned and gave Nicole a sympathetic sigh. "I'll try," she said bravely.

"Thanks," Nicole said, squeezing the older woman's shoulder. "I'll owe you one."

"That will be two you'll owe me," Nancy quipped. "The security people will be on your doorstep Friday morning at nine."

"Thanks twice!" Nicole gave her a quick hug, smiled gratefully, removed her white coat and walked back to her desk where Charlie awaited her. She secured her purse from the bottom drawer and linked her hand in his. "I'm ready," she said, hooking the coat on a rack near the door. Charlie gave her a weak grin and led her out to his new truck. She stepped up on the running board and climbed in, scooting over to the middle so she could sit close to her fiancé.

When Charlie had swung himself up onto the seat, he put the four-wheel drive in gear and steered out of the parking lot, drove around to the front of the building and along Seven Devils Road to Charleston. He parked the car at a festive seaside restaurant known as The Captain's Choice.

Once inside, they sat at a large, overstuffed booth and ordered. Nicole chose a small salmon steak while Charlie decided on a full-course steak dinner. His choice worried her. Charlie once told her he had a ravenous appetite when he was angry or upset. Lately, he'd been on a strict diet, determined to lose ten pounds before their December wedding. He was not what Nicole considered obese, but he was husky.

Charlie was silent throughout their meal and Nicole tried to make polite conversation, but Charlie only grunted or nodded in reply. Between fighting down a sick feeling in her stomach, which was undoubtedly associated with her nausea earlier that day, and worrying about Charlie's withdrawn attitude, she could scarcely eat anything, but pushed her food discreetly around her plate, while watching amicably as Charlie devoured his steak.

Chapter Five

Almost afraid to ask Charlie the reason for his visit, Nicole feared her question would be analogous to setting off a keg of dynamite. For the first time in their relationship, Nicole saw some of the anger Charlie was rumored to harbor.

When they finished eating, Charlie paid the bill and they returned to the truck. He inserted the key into the ignition and Nicole could stand the tension between them no longer. She reached out and touched his hand.

"You're very quiet," she commented, hoping to spur him into conversation.

Charlie nodded toward the Coos River mud flats and observed, "Clammers." His voice was edged with disgust. "Almost as degrading a job as ditch-digging," he insisted. "You'll never see a true fisherman dig clams or ditches . . . or holes they can't wriggle out of." He glared ominously out through the windshield.

Nicole wondered if his insult was directed at the people working in the black mud or at her. She watched an older man out on the river's base, arms sunk into a pre-dug hole, bucket in tow, searching for a large quahog clam, the pride of Charleston. Forcing herself to remain calm and patient, she said, "Please tell me what's wrong, Charlie. I'm not a mind reader."

Turning to face her, Charlie gave her a frown that was unlike the boyish grin to which she was accustomed. Dismally, she realized his anger was directed at her. She could only assume her houseguest had caused his temper to soar, for she had no other secrets from her fiancé.

Finally Charlie growled, "Why did you lie to me?"

Nicole was surprised at the effort it cost him not to explode with the inquiry. "What?" she asked, hoping she misunderstood the question.

He was silent a few more moments as she studied his expression, noting the seriousness of his intent. His explanation came out rapidly. "I asked you several times this morning if everything was all right and you said fine. Was that because you prefer him over me?"

"Who?" she asked, refusing to believe Charlie was speaking about Wade.

"Come off it, Nicole. The man living at your house. You never once mentioned him. When were you planning to tell me?" The torment he felt was expressed on his pallid face and in his angry gray-green eyes.

Nicole inhaled deeply and cast her eyes heavenward. "You mean Wade Reilly?"

"Is that his name?" Charlie asked, placing his hands on the steering wheel, staring straight ahead, as though considering the name very carefully.

"Do you know him?" she questioned.

"No!" he insisted, almost too quickly.

"I can explain," she began. "He's a friend of Danny's."

Charlie glanced at her in surprise. "What's he doing at your place?"

"You remember my telling you Danny wanted a lot of money two weeks ago?" Nicole dreaded every word she must say to try to make Charlie understand.

Charlie nodded but said nothing.

"When I refused to give it to him, he talked Dr. Reilly into loaning it to him. Dr. Reilly now owns Danny's share of the house and Danny's other investments, as well. When I got home from the hospital last night, Dr. Reilly had already settled in."

Charlie was silent for several long minutes, resting his head against his hands on the steering wheel. When he finally spoke, his voice was husky with emotion. "I've been hurt before, Nicole. I couldn't live through another rejection."

For one fleeting moment, Nicole thought she detected a hint of deception in his voice, but she dismissed the thought even as it erupted. She placed her hand upon his neck, massaging a tight muscle. "I know," she whispered. "And I would rather die than hurt you, Charlie, I promise."

"Oh, Babe," he said, pulling her into his arms. "Why do we have to wait until December?"

"We don't have to wait, we can get married Friday if you want. But, you told me you didn't want me to give up my dream of having a winter wedding. I've waited for twenty-nine years for this. Do you really want to give it up?"

"Right now, yes. But two months after the wedding, I'd feel guilty and you know it." He lifted his head and glanced at her with a look of assessment.

"Then we'll wait," she encouraged him. "And everything will work out just perfectly."

"What about this Reilly guy?" he asked. "How long will he be at the house? I don't like him living there, Nicole. Why don't you come and stay aboard my boat until after the wedding?"

"Danny will be home tonight, so I'll be fully chaperoned. Besides, I plan to sell my stocks and buy Danny's portion of the house back."

Charlie frowned. "It's not your responsibility to pay off Danny's debts! And you don't have to live with Reilly for Danny to pay him off!" he yelled. "I won't allow it, Nicole!"

"Charlie!" Nicole exclaimed in shock. Her fiancé had never quarreled with her, nor demanded anything from her before today.

"You heard me," he said, not budging on the issue. "If you don't move out, then I'll move in. Someone has to protect you."

"No!" she said firmly, shaking her auburn curls as she studied her fiancé's reaction. She had never defied Charlie; she had never had any reason to before now. "Let me do this my way," she said, her voice even and steady. "If you don't, I'll think it's because you don't trust me."

Charlie emitted a string of expletives that terrified her. He knew her feelings concerning *gutter words* but he chose to use them, regardless.

Frowning, she said, "I'm right, then. You don't trust me."

"Come off it, Nicole. You know I do. It's just . . . I'm jealous!" he admitted. "What did you expect? A heart of stone?"

"Danny will be there tonight, Charlie. Danny, Mr. Reilly and I have to work this out between the three of us. Please try to understand."

"I don't understand nothing except you've got a man living at your place with you, and you're about to give up your inheritance for a scumbag like your brother!" he yelled, his tone menacingly angry.

"Then try!" she snapped, unwilling to compromise.

Charlie was silent as he turned the key in the ignition. The truck roared to life and Charlie backed out of the parking lot. The wheels made a squealing sound as they raced from gravel to blacktop, heading toward the Institute.

"If you don't slow down around these curves, Charlie, I'm going to be sick!" she complained as her stomach groaned inside her. Nicole looked at herself in the visor's mirror, grateful when Charlie eased the truck's pace. Her once robust, peaches-and-cream complexion was pallid. Her amber brown eyes, made darker by dilated pupils, stared back at her as though she were a stranger. She felt physically ill, lightheaded and queasy.

What was happening to her stable and comfortable world? She and Charlie now had their first argument, her brother had sold half their house and beachfront acreage out from under her, then sent a merciless tyrant to badger her into selling her half. What else could happen to destroy the security she'd known less than twenty-four hours ago?

When Charlie turned the truck into the driveway, he did not park around back, but drove along the oval front. Putting the brake on, he turned off the ignition and pulled Nicole roughly into his arms.

"How did you learn about Wade?" Nicole asked, turning her head before he could kiss her.

"Your brother telephoned me early this morning."

She stared at him in surprise. "Danny called you aboard your boat?"

"On my cell," Charlie nodded. "Said he had called the house several times since three this morning and a man kept answering."

"He knew about Wade all along, and I never heard the phone ring. Not once," Nicole insisted. "Why would Danny say a thing like that?"

"We . . . had an argument before he left for Denver last time," Charlie confessed. "He doesn't like me much. Said he'd bust up our engagement if it was the last thing he did."

"Why didn't you tell me this earlier?" she asked, astounded at her brother's audacity.

"What good would it do?" he questioned. "You two don't get along too well, as it is. I didn't want to add to the problem."

"If he threatened to break us up, why on earth did you believe him?"

"I didn't at first. Although, when you said you were fine, you did seem out of sorts."

"I told you I'm coming down with the flu," she protested, interrupting him.

Charlie shrugged, disregarding her statement. "Well," he continued, "after you left, I telephoned your house and got riled up when I heard a man answer. I drove out to your place. Your friend – "

"Enemy!" she corrected sharply.

Frowning, Charlie said, "He was out running on the beach. Tall, isn't he?"

Nicole nodded and studied Charlie's expression. He seemed wild with jealousy, and barely able to prevent himself from bursting with emotion. Suddenly, his mouth descended on hers, forcing entry. With strong hands, he pressed her tightly against his chest until she could scarcely breathe. For a brief moment, she wondered if she would suffocate first, or be crushed to death under this new and powerful embrace. Fear flooded her. Memories from her past, her first disastrous date, sprang up before her eyes and she suddenly went limp in his arms, telling herself it would be better to give in than to die.

When he finally released her, she gasped, sucking in air and expanding her lungs. "Cha-Charlie!" she stammered, horror evident throughout her trembling body.

"Oh, Babe! I'm sorry," he moaned, gathering her into his arms once more, this time with gentleness. His lips followed the curve of her neck in damp kisses. "Did I hurt you? I'm sorry, Babe. I forgot about what happened before."

Nicole gave him a weak smile but said nothing.

"People are watching," Charlie said, removing his arms and withdrawing from her.

Pulling away, Nicole straightened against the seat of the truck. Doctors Thompson and Reilly were standing twenty feet away on the front steps of the Institute. Her hands went immediately to her bruised lips, where she felt a new puffiness. The taste of blood in her mouth made her stomach churn and she felt more light-headed than ever. She wondered if she would be able to step from the truck without collapsing.

Charlie scowled and opened his door. He hurried around and helped Nicole down from the truck's seat. Placing a kiss on her forehead, he wrapped his hand possessively about her waist.

Grateful for his support, her knees nearly buckled beneath her.

"Miss Travis, aren't we the evasive one today?" Dr. Thompson said in a brisk tone. He observed her kiss-swollen lips and disheveled hair. "I would like to speak with you in my office," he insisted. "I understand you've already met Dr. Reilly, so introductions won't be necessary." Turning abruptly, he preceded them through the front doors.

Nicole noticed Wade's eyes taking in her appearance and missing nothing. He folded his arms and said, "Will you kindly introduce me, Miss Travis!" It was more a demand than a question.

"Yes," she said, hoping the introduction would serve to deflate Wade's ego. "Dr. E. Wade Reilly, I'd like you to meet my fiancé, Charlie Hackett."

"That's encouraging," Wade said with obvious relief. "And when, Mr. Hackett, is the wedding date?"

Nicole frowned. What on earth was Wade doing? Then she remembered his erroneous assumption from earlier that morning. He still thought she was pregnant!

Charlie shuffled his foot against the ground in a penitent gesture, one hand in his pocket, the other still supporting Nicole. "December eighteenth," he said, his voice filled with uncertainty.

"That long?" Wade asked dryly.

Alert and on the defensive, Charlie challenged, "Why not?"

"It's really none of my business," Wade mocked, using Nicole's reiteration from earlier that morning. "I assumed that you would be marrying immediately under the circumstances."

"What are you getting at?" Charlie asked, his temper flaring once again.

Flicking sparks of disgust at Nicole with his callous expression, Wade asked pointedly, "Haven't you told him?"

Nicole rolled her eyes. *This can't be happening*, she thought wearily. She tried to give Wade a rational answer, but she was too dizzy to mouth proper words.

Charlie withdrew his hand from around Nicole's back. He stepped away from her, staring at her with his mouth agape.

"She's pregnant," Wade said. Stepping toward her, a smug smile swept across his face.

An expression of murderous intent filled Charlie's eyes. Nicole trembled violently. She stared from one man to the other, shaken at Wade's outburst yet infinitely aware of Charlie's flash-over anger. The brick-sided Institute building blurred. Faces of the two men, Charlie to her side yet behind her, and Wade standing nearly chest to chest with her, seemed to converge together and spin violently. She stumbled forward, unable to keep her balance, and collapsed unwillingly into Wade's outstretched arms.

Chapter Six

A shrill bell ringing boisterously awakened Nicole. She opened her eyes to find herself lying on the sofa in Dr. Thompson's office. Shadows on the wall told her the sound she'd heard was the last bell of the day. She'd been asleep over two hours. Wearily she sat up and was immediately overcome with nausea. Ignoring Wade and Nancy, who were watching her from across the room, Nicole rushed out through the open door and made a quick dash to the restroom, where she lost her lunch along with all her dignity.

As she washed her hands and face afterward, she realized she was running a slight fever. Nancy Cardston pushed the door open and asked, "Are you all right?" With an air of authority, she walked over to Nicole, letting the restroom door close behind her. She checked

Nicole's pulse, then declared, "A nasty bug. I had it last week, remember?"

Nicole nodded and sank onto a lounge chair.

"You may as well stay home tomorrow," Nancy stated, "and Thursday. By Monday, you'll be good as new."

"Dr. Thompson," Nicole wondered. "He wanted to see me in his office."

Nancy waved her hand in the air with a brushing gesture. "After you fainted, what could he say? He's driven your car back to your home in Bandon-by-the-Sea. His wife will pick him up there. Dr. Reilly will drive you home. You're in no condition to drive today."

"I'm surprised no one called an ambulance," Nicole trembled.

"Dr. Reilly seems to think you're just pregnant, and there's no real cause for alarm." Nancy gave her a curious smile.

"But you don't believe him?" said Nicole, a moment of uncertainty crossing her mind.

"I believe you, dear. I've seen your wrappers in the wastebasket in our shared restroom here at work . . . just last week. It's been too soon to believe anything Dr. Reilly seems to think about you . . . and if you were pregnant, it could only be by a day or two. Morning sickness doesn't usually manifest itself until the fourth week."

Nicole shuddered. Nancy rubbed her shoulder tenderly. "We need to get you home. Dr. Reilly is waiting for you in the hall."

Nodding, Nicole still felt so dizzy she wondered if she would faint again at any moment. Nancy held the door open for her. Weakly, Nicole stood and walked forward, bracing herself against the doorframe.

"Feeling better?" came a familiar voice to her left. She turned and saw Wade coming toward her, a derisive frown on his face. "Here," he said, scooping her up into his strong arms as though she were a small child. "Not too steady on your feet yet, are you?" He carried her out to his white Lexus and placed her in the passenger seat.

Closing her eyes, Nicole recalled with clarity the conversation that had taken place just before she fainted. "I don't like you," she whispered when Wade slid into the driver's seat beside her and had started the car.

"The feeling's mutual, honey," Wade responded. Fortunately, he turned his attention to driving the Lexus back to her home south of Bandon.

Nicole felt that he was deliberately ignoring her. After fifteen minutes of silence, Nicole said,

"You're wrong about me, Wade Reilly. I have the flu. I got it from Nancy, who had it last week. She got it from Dr. Thompson the week before. You'll probably get it yourself next week."

Glancing at her for only a moment, Wade continued driving, refusing to respond. Anger surged up in Nicole's chest as she wondered where Charlie had gone. Why hadn't he stayed to help her get home? Why Wade?

Unable to suppress her anger any longer, she glared at Wade as she snapped, "You've come between me and Charlie Hackett. He'll probably never speak to me again. Why would you do something so hateful?"

When Wade did not respond, tears flooded Nicole's eyes and drizzled down her face. She did not care if he noticed. He had already seen her at her worst. Normally, Nicole rarely cried. Today was different. Charlie had been hurt by Wade's erroneous remark, and had apparently left her at the Institute in Wade's care. What Nicole really needed right now was her father . . . his kind way of tucking her in, bringing her chicken soup, reading favorite magazine articles to her while she tried to rest. But her father was gone. Her plans for a happy life with Charlie had apparently vanished. Nicole's best buddy, Matt Hemsley, was still in the hospital, injured by

burglars. Danny had sold his half of their inheritance without consulting her . . . to a stranger who
was now living with her, and on top of all this, she
was ill with the same stomach flu that had been
sweeping through the Institute for the past two or
three weeks. Miserable, Nicole buried her face in
her hands and wept. Unconcerned how her cheeks
reddened or her eyes puffed when she cried, she
sobbed in uncontrollable gulps.

Finally, Wade pulled the Lexus into her long,
meandering driveway, parked behind a rental car,
which was parked behind her yellow Cooper, and
offered her a handkerchief. Nicole took it from
him in silence and dried her eyes. Silently, she
steeled her nerves and steadied her quivering lips,
then she dashed from the car and into the house
without looking back at Wade Reilly. Not once.

She was unsurprised to see Danny sitting on
the sofa, reading the *Bandon News*. He stood
up quickly, as if to embrace her. "Nicole, Dr.
Thompson said you were sick."

Without speaking to her brother, Nicole fled
to her bedroom, slammed the door shut, stripped
off her clothes, tossed them onto a chair, slipped
into a cotton nightgown, then slid between the
sheets. If anything, her fever was higher than it
had been at the Institute, but at least her stomach didn't ache quite as much. She kicked off

the heavy quilt and bedspread, keeping only the thin cotton sheet over her.

Rolling onto her side, she watched the pine trees outside her window sway back and forth from a light sea breeze. Nicole cracked the window beside the bed open so she could smell the spicy fragrance of three gum-drop shaped myrtlewood trees, perhaps hundreds of years old, that stood between the pines and her house. But, she was too tired to appreciate their unique fragrance. Her eyelids drooped and she slept, only to dream of Wade sitting on her left and Danny sitting on her right. They were both watching over her, one or the other patiently stroking her face with a damp, cool cloth, waiting for her to wake up. Sometimes they were wearing robes and pajamas, other times they were dressed in jeans and tee shirts. At one point, she dreamed she was shivering violently and Wade removed his bathrobe and placed it over her, but she threw it off the moment he left the room. When she struggled to open her eyes, she found herself too exhausted to care, and finally fell back into a deep, healing sleep that lasted nearly thirty-six hours.

By Thursday afternoon she felt better, but she stayed in bed most of the day. Catherine Hemsley, Matt's wife, dropped by with a bowl of hot chicken soup and news of Matt's condition. He would be able to come home in a week, but could do no strenuous activities for a month. Apparently, Claude Browning had telephoned Catherine with news of Nicole's illness.

To Nicole's surprise, Catherine told her she was considering whether or not to hire help for the first few weeks Matt was home. She had prepared the spare bedroom in case she could find a live-in helper. Catherine and Matt owned a mom-and-pop market along Coast 101 where they sold plant stock and most of their farm produce. Until the new police station was built in Bandon, Catherine was the only Notary Public in the area for miles. She always said this public service brought in quite a few sales for their market as well. The market still had the last two weeks of September and all of October to remain open. After Halloween, they usually closed the market and spent the winter in Yuma, Arizona. By mid-March, the Hemsleys always returned to plant their acreage and prepare the market for its annual spring reopening, when fresh tulips and all their seed stock would be ready.

After Catherine's visit, Nicole went back to bed and slept through to the following morning. Wade and Danny had remained helpful but silent regarding the situation they were facing, perhaps waiting until she had recuperated.

On Friday, it seemed apparent to Nicole that she would survive whatever flu she had, and she awakened early. Knotting her bathrobe tightly at her waist, she went into the kitchen prepared for battle. Wade was dressed for work, while Danny was still in his pajamas and robe. They had been whispering before she entered, and their silence at her arrival told her the topic of their conversation was herself.

"I brought you some fresh flowers," smiled Danny, "but they wilted. So I went out yesterday and bought you this silk arrangement." He held up a pale yellow vase with a striking floral bouquet of silk blue wildflowers. "Do you like it?"

"Danny," she said, ignoring the flowers and Wade entirely. "I want to see your copy of the real estate contract between you and Mr. Reilly first thing this morning."

"It's here," said Danny, setting the vase on the table and handing her a large manila envelope by his elbow.

Nicole took the envelope and sat down in the living room. Dumping the contents onto her lap, she found a stack of papers and a smaller envelope that she opened first. It contained an "I'm sorry" card and fifteen hundred dollars in cash. Inside the card, Danny had written:

Dear Sis,

I'm sorry for stealing Mama's jewelry. It was wrong of me, and I have no excuse, except to say I'm sorry. Will you please forgive me? I had planned to buy it back from the pawn shop, but someone (apparently you) beat me to it. When I took the jewelry, I thought you would never even know it was gone. I planned to pay it off and put it back before you ever missed it. That's why I didn't come home this summer. I was too ashamed to tell you the truth. Please forgive me.

Love, Danny

Nicole sighed and whispered to herself, *Oh, Danny. I do forgive you.* Next, she read what appeared to be a standard real estate contract between Wade Reilly and Daniel Travis, with a monthly payment schedule and balloon payment in forty months. Fortunately, Wade had given Danny the right to pay off the loan, provided he did so within three and one-half years. After that time, if Danny could not make the final balloon payment, Danny must forfeit his half of the real estate. Wade had really taken advantage of her brother, for although the loan was high in terms of paying it back, it was perhaps twenty percent of the actual value of Danny's portion of the real estate. Her brother was born a sucker and Wade had somehow manipulated Danny's inheritance into a terrible situation.

Gathering courage, Nicole stuffed the card and cash into her robe pocket and the legal papers back into the envelope. She returned them to her brother and stated authoritatively, "You and I are going down to the bank today, right after the security systems man gets here."

"You're putting in a security system?" Danny asked.

"I am. After nearly shooting your benefactor, I decided it's past time to have one installed. But forgetting about that for the moment, Danny . . . I will sell all my stocks and bonds and loan you the cash you need to pay off your portion of the real estate."

"Until Dan persuades someone else to buy his half of the house again?" Wade questioned. "You won't have any stocks left to sell if you go through with your plan."

Facing Wade squarely, Nicole straightened her shoulders and frowned ominously. "I will write up a contract with Danny. He will not own his portion of the real estate outright, as he has until now. He will have a private mortgage on it, but I will hold the contract and keep it in my safety deposit box at the bank. Danny will make monthly payments on the house for the next ten years with a penalty clause. If he defaults on any two payments, whether separate or consecutively, I will call the loan due. If Danny cannot pay it off, he will lose his share of the house and the two hundred acres to me." Nicole had thought the situation through, and this seemed the best solution to her.

"Having the soft spot you do for your brother, it won't take long before you forgive him and return his share to him free and clear," argued Wade.

"That is none of your affair," she snipped. "My loan to Danny doesn't even remotely concern you."

"Wait a minute," said Danny. "Both of you. I am sitting right here, am I not, listening to all this? Don't I have some say in the matter?"

"You sold your say to Wade," Nicole reminded crossly. "You'll do as you're told."

Shaking his head, Danny said, "I won't accept one dime from your stocks and bonds, Sis. That's your nest egg, and I won't touch it. You're going to have to trust me on this." Danny stood and faced Nicole. "As soon as I get my master's degree, I have a grand job waiting with Schoonaker Pharmaceuticals. I'll be able to send Wade half my income over the next three years, which will pay off my debt to him. At that time, he'll release the real estate contract to me."

"You still have nine credit hours to earn," she protested, thinking how long it had taken him to earn the last five.

"Which I'm finishing up this quarter," Danny insisted. "If I hadn't had to come home this week, it would have been easier; but, if I can get back by Monday, I might still be able to swing it. If not, it will be next quarter before I can finish."

"Then by all means, get back by Monday," said Nicole, feeling defeated. Both men, it seemed, were against her. "But let's get this real estate settled before you go. I don't want Mr. Reilly living here when you leave, Danny. This house was built by Grandpa Travis, and I won't permit it to fall into anyone else's hands."

"I have every right to live here," insisted Wade. "I don't care who built it, right now half of this house is mine."

"Fine!" snapped Nicole. "Then I shall go live with Catherine Hemsley until I can find an apartment to rent. I will not spend one more night with you in my grandfather's house!"

"You cannot move out, Sis!" Danny nearly exploded. "That wasn't my intent. I don't want you living somewhere else. Why can't you get along with Wade?"

Tears gathered thickly in Nicole's eyes, but she forced them back. "It will be difficult enough to work with the insufferable tyrant, Danny, let alone live with him. I couldn't bear it."

"No!" Danny yelled. "Wade! That's not what we agreed upon. You said she could stay here!"

"I'm not pushing her out," Wade argued. "This is her decision."

"Fine!" said Danny, "I'll accept your offer, Sis. Let's go to the bank and cash out your stocks and bonds."

For a moment Nicole thought she saw moisture in Wade's eyes, but when he next spoke, she knew it was greed that she'd seen. "Forget it. I'll buy that motor home I've wanted and live in it. There's a great spot at the northwest corner of our property for a – "

"You can't put a motor home up at Grandpa's Pines!" she shouted. "My grandfather cleared that home site and planted those trees surrounding it when I was five years old. He promised me I could build my house there when I married."

"Are you and Charlie planning to build a house there?" Wade demanded. The volume in his voice had risen to match her temper.

"I haven't told Charlie about it," she confessed, wondering why she hadn't. As if to explain her reasons, she added, "I was waiting for Danny to grow up and make a decision whether he would live here, or build on the southwest corner that Grandpa set aside for him."

A little softer, Wade persuaded, "If you're going to live up there someday, my moving a motor home here will be a great help to you. I'll install a septic system and drill a well big enough for a large family. I'll also have telephone and electricity installed to the site. When you're finally ready to build a home there, all those problems will already be resolved."

Nicole knew what he was saying made sense economically, but it would take away the one place she loved to retreat to when she was troubled or sad. She pouted only for a brief moment, hoping Wade had not noticed.

To persuade her further, Wade added, "I'll install a satellite system so that you can have instant television and internet access when you do build."

Still, Nicole hesitated, thinking of the outcropping of rock upon which she'd sat hundreds of times as she watched the ocean devouring the winter beaches . . . or the gray whales migrating north and south in spring and fall.

Finally, Wade said, "You can come up there anytime you want. I'll even park the motor home toward the back of the lot, behind your grandfather's pine trees, leaving you a clear path to your view of the ocean."

Nicole was amazed that Wade seemed to know what she was thinking, but she dismissed any softness this may have made around the rough edges of his character.

"Please, Sis," coaxed Danny. "You won't even know Wade's living there. We have nearly two hundred acres here. He'll get lost in the forest that far away, and you know it. But if you move out, I – I won't be able to live with myself."

"Oh, now you're threatening suicide?" she demanded. "First gambling, then stealing, then selling my birthright out from under me, and now you plan to take your own life?"

"No, Sis. I've hurt you so much. I can't tell you how sorry I am. But how can I face myself in the mirror every day, thinking I've turned you out of your own home?"

Tears welled up in his eyes, surprising her, but she forced herself to ignore them for the moment. "You should have thought about that before you started gambling again, Danny!" Nicole was not going to let him off so easily. He had to learn that his actions had consequences, and she was caught in the middle of them.

"I've learned my lesson, Sis. You don't have to worry. I'll make good on the loan with Wade.

I swear I will. If I don't, you can have Dad's truck. It's worth more to me than all the real estate, the stocks and the bonds. I'd die before I'd let that truck go."

"Keep the truck," she said, sinking onto a kitchen chair. She looked up at Wade and noticed the tiniest hint of a smile on his lips, though he seemed to be doing a good job of holding it back. Her eyes narrowed as she glared at him. "How soon can you get that motor home here?"

"I can go into Eugene and pick it out today. Would tomorrow be too soon?" he asked.

"No, that's fine," Nicole answered. "In the meantime, I'll borrow Matt's road plow and clear the road of undergrowth for you. I cleared it last spring, but it's overgrown again."

"No need," said Wade. "I'll hire a grader and have a nice blacktop put down for us. No more plows needed."

"Fine. Tell them I don't want a single tree injured. Most of those pines were planted by my Grandpa Travis." Turning to Danny, Nicole said, "Haven't you got a plane to catch back to Denver?"

Danny squatted down to face her, and looked up into her brown eyes. Taking both of her hands in his, he said, "I was sort of hoping I could fly back on Sunday. Maybe you'd like to spend the day with me tomorrow, if you're feeling better. Perhaps we could rent a couple of horses and spend low tide on the beach. I'll make some hoagies and you can bring some of your home-made apple juice."

Nicole closed her eyes and shook her head. What was she to do with her brother? He was such a smooth talker, and she a pushover. "If I'm feeling better," she agreed. "But right now, I'm going to take a long, luxurious bath."

Pulling her up into his arms, Danny gave her a lengthy hug. "Everything will work out okay, Sis. I know it will."

"We shall see, Danny." She kissed him on the cheek and whispered, "Make sure Dr. Reilly's gone before I get out of the tub. I wouldn't care if he never darkened my door-step again."

Nodding, Danny released her. Refusing to speak another word to Wade, Nicole turned into the living room and walked down the hall and into the bathroom. After closing the door, she heard the two men talking in unintelligible whis-pers for several minutes. Then she heard some-one packing a suitcase in Danny's bedroom, foot-steps that went back down the hall and out through the kitchen. The side door closed and the Lexus roared to life. Nicole could only hope that Wade would be true to his word.

She was bathed, dressed and scrubbing down the bathroom when the security systems men arrived. By four that afternoon, they had installed a state-of-the-art system that no burglar could get by. They even had her code in her own password so that no one, not even Danny, could get into her house without her permission. Within five seconds, an alarm would go off at OCA Headquarters, and a call to the police department would bring help to her within five minutes. For the first time in her life, Nicole was glad Bandon-by-the-Sea had built the new police station at the southern edge of town.

No more burglars for Nicole. Now, if she could just get rid of Wade Reilly as easily.

Chapter Seven

The sun danced through the water's curl, making it look like pale, opaque sheers of the most beautiful aquamarine Nicole had ever seen as wave after wave coiled forward toward the beach. Sand crabs scurried out of the path of the horses' hooves, as Nicole and Danny trotted their steeds toward the Garden of the Gods along Oregon's rugged coastline. Passing in Face Rock's shadow, they continued until they reached the driest portion of beach and dismounted. While Nicole spread a blanket on the damp sand, Danny tied the horses to a hitching post nearby that had been installed by Bandon's city fathers a few years earlier.

Monster hoagy sandwiches were lifted from the basket, along with a thermos filled with cold, fresh apple juice. Danny had even brought the yellow vase with blue silk flowers to brighten

Nicole's spirits. To her amazement, Danny entertained Nicole most of the day, recalling to her mind memories of their childhood and the ways they used to tease their father. Dad always loved a good laugh, and with two young rascals under his care, there were ample opportunities to make him roar with laughter.

Finally, Danny had talked himself out of topics. They were both full of food, and they stretched out on their backs in the bright sunshine. Nicole knew this was her time to talk. Whenever they spent the day together, the first half was always Danny's allotted time to tell her everything. For reasons known only to himself, he had spent the morning making Nicole laugh. Her part, during the second half, was always more serious, and Danny seemed to have sensed this need before they rented their horses.

Nicole remained silent for about fifteen minutes, letting the warmth of the afternoon sun seep into her soul, bolstering her courage. When she could wait no longer, she sat up and voiced her concerns, keeping her tone level and restrained.

"Danny, how did you ever meet up with Dr. Reilly?" she asked at length.

"I met his cousin a while back. She's a sweet woman who lives her life in a wheelchair. She introduced us."

"Really?" she said. "Does his cousin go to the University at Denver?"

"No, actually she lives in Denver, but she used to live in Astoria, Oregon. But how we met is not the important issue. You want to know how it is that I sold my birthright to Wade."

"Yes," she admitted. "I would."

Danny hesitated a moment, as if gathering courage himself. Finally, he said, "When I phoned you a few weeks ago to ask to borrow money, it wasn't for a gambling debt, Nicole. I wanted to help fund a charitable project that I discovered through my studies at the University. I donated most of what I borrowed from Wade to a worthy cause."

"Hmmpf," she smiled, unable to prevent an outburst of laughter. "That'll be the day."

"No, really," he said. Sitting up, he reached out and took her hand in his. He rubbed her fingers back and forth as their father used to do, and Nicole noticed a tear slip down the his face and drip from his chin. "I met the kindest, most beautiful woman, Nicole. Her name's Ella Schoonaker. She introduced me to the charity. We're trying to push for more grants and better care of our paraplegics."

"So you expect me to believe you used all the money Wade loaned you for a charity?" she asked, unable to trust him.

"I've changed," persuaded Danny. "Last year when I stole Mama's jewelry from you, that was the lowest point in my life. I reached rock bottom, Sis. I admit that I stole the jewelry to repay a gambling debt. When I couldn't purchase the jewelry back, I went into a deep depression. Ella brought me out of it. She noticed I had been missing classes, and she tracked me down. I was drunk the day she arrived, trying to drown my sorrows in a bottle of gin. I was a wreck. She pulled me through it, got me going back to classes, helped me get a temporary position at Schoonaker Pharmaceuticals – her dad owns the company – and then she showed me how three percent of their profits go into paraplegic research. Her mother is paraplegic, by the way. Injured her spinal cord in a car accident. She's how I met Wade's cousin."

"Are you serious about this Ella?" Nicole asked, praying with all her heart and soul that she could be the one woman to tame her wayward brother.

"I want to marry her," he admitted. "But I don't dare ask her yet. I get the feeling that her father expects someone a little more stable than me."

"That's why you're working harder on your studies?"

Danny nodded. "I have to get my master's degree because it will land me a good promotion in the company. Mr. Schoonaker says he'll advance anyone willing to get their master's degree on their own. If they succeed, he'll finance the rest of their schooling so they can pull in a doctorate and work in his research lab. That's where I'm headed. Once I've established myself in the doctorate program, I'll have some hope that her father won't bounce me out on my ear."

Nicole laughed. "A doctorate, Danny? Are you serious? Or are you really trying to tell me you sold Dr. Reilly your real estate holdings in order to show off to Ella's father, pretending that you're a big philanthropist by bolstering his wife's cause?" she guessed wisely.

"A little *act* of kindness never hurt anything," Danny insisted.

"Oh, Danny! Can't you see how wrong that is? You're trying to buy Mr. Schoonaker's approval of you, and you're going into debt to do it."

"I had to, Nicole. I can't afford to lose Ella. She means the world to me." He leaned forward and grinned at her. "I want to bring her home for Christmas this year. Do you think that would be all right?"

"Of course," Nicole said. "But when she finds out you hocked your inheritance to buy her father's approval, how is she going to feel?"

"She won't care, Sis. Ella understands me. I think she's falling for me, too. Besides, she's got more money than you, me and Wade put together. It's not the money. Don't you see? It's getting on her father's good side up front. If all goes well, we'll get married long before I need to pay the balloon payment to Wade."

"What if your plan sours?" Nicole asked, forcing him to face the severe consequences of his actions.

"If things go poorly between Ella and my-self, which I really don't see happening, I'll still have my income to fall back on. The company pays those with master's degrees four times what we with bachelor's degrees make, for doing the same job and putting in the same amount of time. The day I have my degree in my hand, my in-come quadruples. It will be easy to pay more than half of it to Wade, and still have more money left over than I'm making right now."

"I hope you're right," Nicole said, squeez-ing his hand. "So tell me how Dr. Reilly entered the picture."

"His cousin introduced us. We became friends. He makes a hefty income from his textbooks and he does seminars all around the country. I led him to believe that I had some gambling debts I wanted to pay off– "

"You lied to him?" she asked.

"No, it wasn't really a lie. I am gambling. I'm gambling my inheritance on pleasing Ella's father, smoothing the way for us. It's a big gamble I'm taking, but she's worth every penny."

"That's the problem, then, isn't it?" Nicole grimaced. "If you never pay Dr. Reilly back, he gets your inheritance and that leaves me half owner of our grandfather's property with a stranger. You have no consequences to pay for your lack of judgment, but I do. I stand to lose everything."

"But Wade wouldn't– "

"He was perfectly willing to let me move out yesterday, before you insisted that I shouldn't," she pointed out.

"No, Sis. You can trust Wade. He would never hurt you."

"There are many forms of pain, brother dear. He doesn't have to hit me to hurt me. Do you want to know where I see this situation headed?"

Danny shrugged. "You have to trust him, Sis."

"Danny, I see four years into the future. You haven't paid the loan and it'll be called due. Dr. Reilly won't accept my money, only yours. You have no money and you refuse to let me sell my stocks and bonds. Dr. Reilly owns his half of the house and the property and I'm forced to sell my half to him just to keep the peace. Can you honestly not see that happening?"

"At least you would still have your investments," Danny insisted. "You could sell them and buy a beautiful home near Charleston."

"I shouldn't have to sell them. I shouldn't have to leave the home our grandfather built. I shouldn't be forced to abandon the home our father left us. Your life will turn out rosy working for Schoonaker with your mighty master's degree, while mine will go down the sewer."

"No, you'll marry Charlie and go fishing every day just like you want. You'll be happy no matter where his boat lands."

Accepting the change in topic, Nicole said, "In case you hadn't noticed, Charlie hasn't called once since I got sick. We were supposed to go fishing today, but in light of what happened at work, I suppose Charlie wants to break up with me."

"Why?"

"Dr. Reilly told Charlie that I'm pregnant, and Charlie knows it couldn't be his child."

"Are you?" Danny asked.

She almost smacked him, but restrained her-self. "Danny, I– I've never–" she stammered. "I'm still a virgin."

"That's more than I needed to know," he said, blushing, standing up and gathering their glasses, flowers and sandwich wrappings into the basket.

"Well, you asked!" she retorted, shaking the blanket out. She folded it roughly and handed it to him.

As she put a foot in the stirrup and mounted her horse, Danny said, "Is this because of what happened back when you were sixteen?"

Nicole cringed, but nodded briefly. "I guess so." It wasn't exactly true. She had only found one man who could tempt her, and she considered him com-pletely out of bounds. Nicole would never allow herself to fall for a man like Wade Reilly.

Soon they were headed back along the beach. Nothing had been resolved in Nicole's mind. Her brother had everything going for him, while her world would come crashing down around her.

When Danny challenged her to a race, she accepted and yelled, "Heeyah!" spurring her steed forward. It was never difficult to outrace Danny, no matter what horses they rode, and today was no different than a thousand such challenges. Danny just didn't have the drive she did. He let problems slip past him without worrying about them, while she worked tirelessly to solve them, to get ahead of the trials and put them past her as quickly as possible. She could only pray that her efforts would pay off this time as well.

That evening, Wade arrived with a brand new thirty-six foot motor home he had bought from a dealer in Eugene, Oregon. He would have to park it in her driveway until the road contractor put in the new road out to Grandpa's Pines. Danny invited Wade to supper, much to Nicole's dismay, but she didn't want to be rude, so she let the two men prepare supper out on the deck while she took a hot shower. By the time she had pampered herself into the amazingly beautiful woman she really was, the men were taking three steaks off the grill. The round, wooden table was covered with a fresh tablecloth and wild flowers stood in a small burgundy-colored vase in the center. The men had also prepared a fresh fruit salad and corn on the cob.

Nicole was careful to keep her conversation light and gracious, praying in her heart that Danny and Wade would stick to their plans. It would not do to antagonize Wade any further, especially since she would be working with him beginning Monday at the Marine Institute at Charleston.

Shortly after supper, the telephone rang. Nicole grabbed the deck phone and answered, "Travis residence."

"It's me," came the familiar voice of her fiancé.

"Oh, Charlie," she said. "I'm glad you called."

"I think we should talk," Charlie said. "I want to know what's going on."

"Why don't you come over?" she suggested. "I'm feeling much better now."

"I'll be right over." He hung up the line without saying goodbye.

Nicole replaced the receiver and turned around. Both men were looking at her with danger flashing from their eyes. She ignored their mutinous expressions and said, "You'll have to clean up. Charlie's coming over and I want to change into something I know he'll like."

"What?" demanded Wade, a look of incredulity upon his handsome face. "What's wrong with the clothes you're wearing?"

"What does it matter to you?" she asked, crinkling her forehead in a frown. "How I dress has nothing to do with you."

"I'll clear," said Danny.

"I'll go get my gun," said Wade.

"But you told me you don't make it a habit to shoot game in any form," Nicole teased, wondering why Wade seemed to hate Charlie so. Then she realized that he still thought she was pregnant with Charlie's baby. Surely Danny would have told him the truth by now. Don't men tell each other all the juicy details?

"In his case, I'll make an exception." Wade stormed off to his motor home.

"You told Wade I'm not pregnant, didn't you?" she whispered to Danny.

"Nope. None of my business." Her brother scooped up a handful of dishes and headed toward the kitchen door.

Nicole held the door open for him, then went back to her bedroom where she dressed in a pair of cream-colored knickers and a cinnamon-colored blouse. Her reflection in the mirror made her smile. The knickers molded to her hips, betraying the little-girl-lost image she tried to capture. She had worn this same outfit for Charlie before and he had commented how much he liked it. *It makes me want to protect you and ravish you all at the same time* he had admitted. The next night Charlie had proposed to her. It was an outfit that had already had a favorable impact on him, and she hoped that they could work out their problems once she told him that she certainly was not pregnant.

"Sis," said Danny as she came out of the bedroom, "I'm going over to Grandpa's Pines to show Wade where you'll want the road."

"Okay."

"You going to make up with Charlie?" he asked.

"I hope so. Once Charlie learns that I'm not pregnant, we should be able to behave like adults and talk things over."

Danny went to the front window and opened the drapes. "When we get back, we'll see if it's safe to come in. We can discreetly look through the front windows. That way we won't disturb you two if you're in a hot embrace."

Nicole blushed. "I won't let it go that far, Danny. You should know that by now."

"You never know," he grinned. "He could change your mind."

"He doesn't have a chance," she confessed. "He still owes me an apology for his behavior in his truck the day I fainted at work."

"Hmm," he mused aloud. "You want me to stay and protect you?"

"I think I can handle Charlie," she assured him. "Now, go. Will you?"

"Sure. Dishes are in the dishwasher. See you later." He gave her a kiss on the cheek. "Bye."

Nicole watched him leave, then returned to her bedroom where she finished brushing her hair. When she heard the front door click shut, she called out, "Charlie? Is that you?"

"No, it's just your friendly neighborhood burglar," Wade said from the entry.

Nicole walked into the living room to find Wade switching on both lamps. "I thought you were going with Danny up to Grandpa's Pines."

"His girlfriend called on his cell phone. I expect he'll be a while."

"You know I'm expecting Charlie?" she asked, irritated that Wade had come into the house without knocking, like he owned the place.

Wade looked her up and down, anger glinting from his blue eyes. "Rather juvenile attire for a woman who's about to face the firing squad at the hands of her fiancé, isn't it?" he asked, frowning at her choice of clothes. His face was dark with animosity and a muscle twitched along his jaw.

Nicole felt disappointed that Wade did not approve, so she retaliated by matching his sarcasm. "This is not your home," she insisted.

"Yet!" he growled. Crouching down, Wade placed kindling and tinder in the fireplace, then lighted it with a match.

"I would like some privacy when Charlie gets here," she said, her hands knotting into fists at her sides.

"Don't worry. I won't even be noticed." He placed a few small split logs in the fireplace, arranging them apart for better air circulation.

"I don't like you," Nicole confessed, refusing to allow any other feelings to bubble to the surface.

"So you said," he responded. When Wade stood, he walked menacingly toward her, his height dwarfing her, making her feel like a small child in comparison.

What would he do to punish her insolence? Kiss her? Nicole felt her cheeks crimson at the thought. She kept her eyes upon a pattern in the carpet, rather than look up at him and renew the feelings she'd had their first evening together. When his shoes were less than an inch from her own, she knew she would never win any battle against him, emotional or otherwise. She couldn't stop her heart from beating for Wade Reilly, no matter how hard she tried. Slowly, she lifted her eyes until she could fix her gaze on a button of his blue shirt level with his chest.

With gentleness, he tilted her head up and forced her to look at him. His eyes were dark with emotion. Was it desire? Could he possibly feel anything like she did? Her heart pounded fiercely inside, threatening to burst with excitement at his nearness.

"You'll soon discover that I'm moody," he whispered. His voice was deep and husky. "Selfish, demanding, arrogant, and right now . . . ." His eyes roved over her face, not missing the desire in her expression or the quivering of her lower lip. With his finger, he traced the outline of her mouth, heating her lips until they ached with longing. Then he bent, lowering his lips within an inch of hers. His eyes darkened and held her gaze.

Suddenly he straightened, turned away and walked over to the open window.

"What's wrong?" Nicole asked, bewildered that he had stopped himself from kissing her. When he did not answer, and without thinking through the consequences of such a question, she asked again, "What's wrong?"

"Nothing," he muttered, staring silently into the darkening night.

"Something's wrong," she blurted out. "What did I do?"

"You?" He turned and gave her a crooked smile. "It's not you, Nicole. It's me."

Timidly Nicole stepped toward him. "Why?" she asked recklessly. He stretched out his hand, beckoning her to come to him. Eagerly she accepted, placing her hand in his, walking close enough that their bodies touched. Tilting her head back to study his serious expression, she repeated the question, "Why?" Her eyes misted with uncertainty.

"I have no right to want you like I do," he whispered.

His words sounded like music to Nicole's ears. Her eyes widened and she wondered if she had heard correctly.

Wade nodded in answer to her unspoken question as he caressed her cheek with curled fingers. "What you do to me, Nicole. I couldn't begin to tell you."

Nicole trembled. Her heart thumped so fiercely she wondered if he could hear it. Her eyes riveted to his lips, full and inviting.

Placing his hand under her chin, he tilted her head and bent slowly toward her until his mouth touched hers. Gently he kissed her, deepening the embrace only when she was ready.

Her thoughts reeled in her head, keeping pace with the rapid beating of her heart. She parted her lips, eagerly repeating the movements of his mouth upon hers, following his example. Wade was a superb teacher, Nicole a willing pupil.

Molten desire flamed her senses and she leaned against him to steady herself. His arms wrapped about her and drew her nearer. She arched forward, feeling the imprint of his body against her.

Then, gently but with no apparent reason, he released her and pushed her away, his mouth withdrawing reluctantly from hers. A look of pain crossed his face and Nicole winced in reaction. "What is it?" she whispered.

"A car is sitting in the driveway," he said. "It must be your fiancé, Charlie Hackett."

Chapter Eight

"Oh!" Nicole moaned aloud, her hand automatically touching her kiss-swollen lips.

"I'll leave you two alone," Wade said, his voice husky and poignant. "I'm sorry I took advantage of you like that, Nicole. You belong to Charlie." Removing his hands from her shoulders, he gave her a sad, almost sardonic smile and sauntered down the hall to the bathroom.

His words penetrated straight to her heart. *You belong to Charlie.* How could she have responded to Wade's amorous advances as though Charlie didn't even exist? Her cheeks reddened with increasing remorse. All those months she had spent convincing Charlie of her faithfulness, and she'd practically abandoned herself to another man, one she scarcely knew.

Hurriedly, Nicole glanced at her reflection in the mirror. She didn't appear any different.

Silently, Nicole prayed Charlie had not seen Wade kiss her through the living room window. Why had Danny opened the drapes? Why?

The doorbell rang. Nicole inhaled and put on a pleasant smile before opening the door.

Charlie stood on the front porch, his hat in his hand, wearing a dashing suit and matching tie. It was so out of character that Nicole nearly burst into laughter, but stopped herself in time.

"Come in," she entreated. "I'm glad you came, Charlie."

He did not answer, but followed her into the living room where he sat opposite her on the sofa. Charlie's expression was livid, that much was obvious from the grim set of his jaw and his glaring, hate-filled eyes. From their earlier telephone conversation, she had expected him to be penitent. But he wasn't.

"I want my ring back," he said, his voice harsh.

"What?" Nicole asked, surprised at the brutality in his tone.

"You heard me." He rolled the rim of his hat with his fingers, squeezing it until his knuckles were white. The action led Nicole to believe he would have preferred to be squeezing her neck in the same manner. She shivered in horror with the thought.

"The wedding is off," he continued. "I'll send you a bill for my labor on your house."

"Then I'm guilty before proven innocent, is that it?" she asked, angry that he should be so callous and insensitive.

"After what I've just seen, I don't need no more proof," Charlie told her. "The way I see it, you're playing us both for fools."

"What?" Nicole was confused at his statement.

"That's right. I watched you kissing him through the window. There you were for the whole world to see. Is it his child, Nicole? You know it's not mine!"

Nicole shook her head in disbelief. She had never seen Charlie this upset before. But she was far more upset that Charlie could believe Wade's lies, rather than the truth he must have found in her somewhere in the past six or eight months.

Charlie stood up, put the hat on his head and pounded his hand with a tight fist. "It doesn't matter. You'll find some other bleeding heart to marry you." Violence was written all over his angry face.

For the second time in their relationship, Nicole was afraid of Charlie. "Since you don't trust me," she said, standing and walking toward the front door, "you're obviously not the man I thought you were. Here." Angrily she turned and twisted the engagement ring off her finger, holding it out to him.

With one swift motion, he followed Nicole to the door and slapped her hand, sending the ring flying across the room where it landed beneath the kitchen table. "I ought to kill you!" he rasped. "Playing me for a fool! You must think I'm an idiot, expecting me to believe you've had a premature baby when the kid arrives less than nine months after we marry!"

"I've heard enough," Nicole said, surprised at how calm her voice sounded when inside she was screaming. She opened the front door for him. "Perhaps one day you'll apologize."

"For trusting you in the first place? Never!" he growled, pushing the door shut. He stepped toward her and wrapped his vise-like hands around her upper arms, squeezing until she thought they would break.

"Charlie!" she gasped. "You're hurting me!"

"Not as bad as I'm gonna'!" he threatened.

"Did Charlie leave, honey?" Wade called. The bathroom door opened and Wade walked down the hall, shirtless, with the top button of his levis undone.

Nicole's eyes widened in surprise.

"Did you see where I put my bathrobe?" Wade asked, walking under the archway into the living room.

Charlie dropped his hands to his sides while Nicole massaged her upper arms tenderly.

"Oh! Sorry," Wade said. "Thought you'd be gone by now. Excuse me, honey. I'll look for my robe in your bedroom."

Charlie turned to leave. "You'll be sorry for this, Nicole!" he warned as he slammed the door shut and left.

Nicole leaned her forehead against the frame. "Why?" she whispered to herself. "Why?"

"Because I wanted to catch him off guard," Wade answered behind her.

Nicole swung around. "You've been eavesdropping the whole time," she accused. "Why?"

"It's a good thing!" Wade protested. "I'll be surprised if you don't have bruises on both your arms by morning. What kind of man were you engaged to?"

"I don't know," she whimpered. "He never hurt me before you showed up!" Nicole leaned against the door, trying to remember happier times with Charlie. "He was always kind and gentle . . . and he loved me. Why couldn't you just leave well enough alone?"

"Nicole!" Wade scolded. Then his tone changed to tender persuasion as he stepped near her. "Can't you see I was only – "

"Don't — don't you *Nicole* me!" she snapped. Racing past him, she fled to her bedroom where she slammed the door and collapsed onto the bed.

"Nicole!" Wade called through her closed door. "I was only trying to protect you. Your Charlie must be a woman-beater if he can bruise you like he did! Can't you see that?"

"He was hurt!" she insisted, trying to rationalize Charlie's behavior. "How would you feel if you were Charlie?"

"I certainly wouldn't threaten you! I would never hurt you."

"Oh, that's right. You're Mr. Perfect!" she returned sarcastically. "Then why am I hurting, Wade? Isn't this what you wanted all along?"

"Nicole," he said, his voice held a trace of remorse. "I didn't want to hurt you. What do you want me to do? Tell me how I can help you?"

"If you really wanted to help me, you would go after Charlie and tell him you were mistaken, and that I'm not pregnant!"

"Would that be the truth?" he asked timidly.

Nicole opened her mouth to give him an angry retort. But it wasn't worth the effort. Wade apparently did not believe her. Why should she bother to correct him? He would know the truth nine months from now, and then he would have to apologize. "Go away!" she moaned. "I don't know how you expect me to like you when you deliberately try to destroy everything I care about!"

After a while Nicole heard his footsteps recede down the hall. Wearily, she pressed her head against the pillow. She was more disappointed by Wade's actions than by Charlie's manhandling her. Wade's behavior seemed so deliberate somehow. Why had he come out of the bathroom calling her endearing names, insinuating that his bathrobe was in her bedroom. He didn't have to go to such lengths to rescue her from Charlie's grip. A simple stroll into the room, fully clothed and disinterested, would have accomplished the same purpose.

Nicole rolled over and dangled an arm off the bed, feeling as limp as a rag doll. Instead of her hand touching the carpet as she had anticipated, she felt a smooth piece of fabric she had not expected. Leaning over, she saw a crumpled Egyptian cotton bathrobe, a man's bathrobe, blue with a white border.

Disbelieving her eyes, Nicole picked it up. It was Wade's, of that she was certain, but what was it doing in her bedroom? She hugged it against her, recalling the evening of her illness when she had dreamed Wade sat by her bedside. Perhaps it wasn't a dream, after all, and that thought confused her. If Wade sat beside her while she was so ill, it would indicate that he cared about her, at least a little. The thought that Wade actually cared about her, even in the least degree, not only worried her, but it made Nicole giddy with happiness. That night she found sleep a fleeting experience.

Around eight the following morning, Danny knocked on her bedroom door. "Sis," he called softly.

Nicole rolled over. "I'm awake. Come in."

Danny entered, placed the burgundy vase, now filled with small silk flowers, atop her dresser. Then, he sat down on the side of her bed. "Rough night?" he asked. "You look miserable."

"That bad, hmm?"

"Dark circles," he said. "You should probably sleep longer. Wade's going to take me to the airport up at North Bend. He'll be back later."

"Why don't you return the rental car?"

"It won't start. It's a rental, what can I say? I called the company and they're sending a tow truck to pick it up."

"Tell Wade I'm not pregnant," pleaded Nicole.

"He doesn't believe me," said Danny. "I tried to tell him last night, but he wonders now if the father is Claude Browning's."

"Claude's a married man and he adores Margo. I would never date someone else's husband! What is wrong with Wade?" she asked. "He is the most pig-headed, obstinate, arrogant man I've ever – "

"All of the above," said Danny with a tender smile. He bent over and kissed her forehead. "Keep your prayers said for Ella and me," he requested.

Nicole nodded. "Bye," she said, pulling him close and loving the clean smell of him. Danny's scent reminded her so much of their father she always gave him an extra long hug whenever he left. Any other resemblance to their father, she never noticed, for Danny was the male version of her lovely mother. "Sorry for getting so upset with you."

"I deserved it," he admitted. "Bye."

When she heard Wade's Lexus pull away from the driveway, Nicole snuggled deeply under the blankets and fell asleep. It wasn't until almost eleven in the morning when she awakened. Quickly, she straightened the house, put Wade's robe on a hanger in Danny's closet, and plastered the bullet hole in the wall above the door frame in the living room. Afterward, she went outside to weed the garden and gather in a basket of fresh beets.

After eating a late lunch, she changed into her swimsuit and wrapped a sarong around her waist. Munching on an apple, Nicole walked past three myrtlewood trees clumped together like gigantic, fat gumdrops, their glossy, pointed leaves eminating a spicy, laurel-like fragrance that followed her upon a light breeze down the trail to the beach. The path was surrounded by tall grand fir and Douglas pine. Bushy huckleberry plants clamored for sunlight along with the Salix willows. Deeper in the forest, Nicole could see clumps of wood sorrel and deer ferns. Occasionally, she would stop to admire a tall redwood tree boxed in by Sitka spruce. Soon the spruce population diminished, replaced by salt brush and sand. The sun was still warm and prominent in the western sky. Nicole guessed she had about four hours of daylight left, the perfect time for tanning and not burning.

Before long, Nicole was stretched out on her belly upon a beach blanket. From her viewpoint, she could see a majestic kingfisher circle and dive for food, its white and black feathers hugging its graceful body. The kingfisher's symmetrical movement was rivaled by none. Its mighty wings permitted it to soar upward to dizzying heights, then plunge seaward in a spiraling symphony of beauty.

Monstrous waves crashed and thundered against the ever-changing coastline. Not a swimming beach, Nicole was well aware of strong undercurrents waiting just beneath the break line to snare anything that ventured into its path. The dangers inherent did not alter the beauty and mastery of the swelling, cresting waves, curling toward the beach with mammoth strength.

A shadow fell across her and Nicole looked up . . . way up to see Wade standing above her like a sentinel in the afternoon sun.

"Your Charlie put out to sea," Wade told her as he sat down beside her on the sand, his denim-clad legs just inches from her bare, slender, tan legs. "It's probably just as well. Nothing I could have said would alter his opinion. He seems as stubborn and bullheaded as– "

"You," she finished for him.

"Lets not generate another argument," he suggested, staring down at her slim body absorbing the sun's rays.

Nicole nodded and turned onto her back. She watched his eyes rove over her arms and legs, her skin covered only by her swimsuit. Wade did not miss a thing, she decided.

When he finished studying her, he stretched out on the sand beside her, his head cradled in his hands. The thought of Nicole so near was like fire in his blood, a devouring Oregon flame that drove out all other thoughts. Even with his eyes closed, he could picture her beauty, soft and warm, yet vibrant and alive. Her hair, a chestnut waterfall of curls around her head and shoulders, framed the delicate bronze-tone of her beautiful face. Her lips, heart-shaped, held the promise of an all-consuming wildfire. Her brown eyes, light yet deep, filled him with a sensation of drowning whenever he studied them. Nicole's petite body was lithe, firm yet softly woman in every detail.

Nicole seemed different from any other woman he had ever known. She confused him and enslaved him with a tantalizing fire that only she could assuage.

While his eyes were closed, Nicole rolled onto her side so she could observe Wade. Compared to her, his height seemed massive. His broad shoulders were well-muscled, though not overly so. He had a lean waist, strong thighs, high cheekbones, a squarish chin and dark eyebrows. His dark brown hair he wore natural with waves across the crown and modest curls at the nape.

When Wade opened his eyes, they locked with hers. At that very moment, Nicole felt lost. One moment she was wondering if she should respond to his obvious admiration, and the next instant she was marveling how extraordinarily handsome he was with that expression he had that made her feel thoroughly desirable.

The world around her blurred and all she could see was Wade looking at her with a hungry glitter in his eyes. It was as though nothing existed but Wade. The kingfisher seemed to hold its place in the sky. The mighty waves stopped in mid-crush, halting right at their most magnificent crest, as though waiting for this moment to pass. All sound vibrated into a silence that transcended any other calm on earth.

Wade lifted his hand, his fingers slowly drawing an imaginary arc across her cheek to her chin. Methodically he retraced their course, again and again.

Without conscious thought, Nicole placed her fingers upon his lips and traced their outline. Immediately her fingertips warmed, spreading heat from the point of contact.

His lips drew nearer hers, their eyes locked as though magnetized to each other. She had never wanted any man to kiss her as eagerly as she wanted Wade. He stopped less than an inch from her mouth. Time seemed to stand still as he smiled down at her.

Nicole stretched her fingers through his hair, pulling him closer until his lips united with hers, generating an aching sensation in her lower abdomen unequaled by any other. She was caught in his web, in the magical spell of desire he cast upon her.

Suddenly, sand was splattered across them as a beach ball landed nearby. Children had come onto the beach and were splashing in the shallow waves.

Their moment together ended. Wade sat up. The kingfisher soared again, the waves crashed against the beach, pounding their perpetual chant of new beginnings. Children laughed and called to one another.

Quickly, Wade stood and tossed the ball to a freckle-faced boy, one Nicole recognized as a grandchild of Matt and Catherine Hemsley. She could only watch and listen and think. What had she been doing? She hardly knew Wade, yet she had been willing to give herself to him. What was wrong with her? Wade could not become her lover. Wade was her enemy.

Chapter Nine

After Nicole warned the children not to go more than ankle-deep into the water, Catherine Hemsley arrived. Nicole had no further reason to remain on the beach so she wrapped the sarong around her waist and tied it securely. Then she picked up her beach blanket, shook it, folded and tucked it under her arm, and without another word to Wade, headed for the path leading home.

He followed her in silence.

When she reached the deck, the telephone was ringing. Quickly, she stepped up the redwood stairs and answered. "Travis residence."

Claude Browning's voice sounded rushed and frantic. "Miss Travis, we have eight pilot whales beached at Bullards. Three of them are still alive. Hurry."

"I'll be right there." She hung up the phone and turned to Wade. "We have stranded whales on Bullards Beach."

"I'll go with you," he insisted.

"We could use you," she admitted. "Give me a few seconds to throw some clothes on."

Wade nodded. "I'll meet you at my car."

"No, let's take mine," she insisted. "The local police will never let you through. They'll think you're a tourist. They know my little Cooper."

"Good plan."

Nicole left him standing there and rushed into the house. Quickly she pulled on a pair of shorts and a tee shirt, leaving on her swimsuit. She grabbed two bottles of Gatorade from the fridge, a clean pair of sweats and two towels, then dashed to the car and found Wade already standing beside the yellow Mini Cooper, waiting for her to unlock the door. He had a large duffle bag with him.

Within moments, they were headed north on Coast 101 towards Bandon-by-the-Sea. After crossing the Coquille River, they turned onto the road leading to Bullards Beach State Park. Cars were parked everywhere along the side, and Nicole drove around these to the head of the line, honking her horn the entire way.

When she pulled up next to the police barricade, an older officer leaned down and smiled. "Evening, Miss Travis. We can take you the rest of the way in the buggy."

"Thanks, Henry. This is Dr. Wade Reilly. He's a marine biologist– "

"I know who he is. Welcome, Dr. Reilly. I expect we'll need all the help we can get." To Nicole, he added, "Just park your Cooper up at the front and I'll radio Jonah to come pick you up."

Several minutes later, they found themselves atop a massive dune machine that could traverse the sand dunes without any difficulty. Jonah Johnson, a fairly new recruit to the beach security force, drove the "buggy" northward about two miles, where they were let off and greeted by Dr. Thompson. Beyond him were Claude Browning and nearly every staff member and student from the Institute, already at work trying to save the whales.

Eight pilot whales lay stranded upon the beach. The tide was going out, and Nicole realized they would be hard-pressed to save any of them. Already, three large tractors waited on the beach with slings hanging from tall towers jury-rigged atop them. Blood from the deceased whales stained the beaches below them and the water foamed red. Immediately, Nicole saw that four of the five dead whales had been slashed by sharks. The largest whale, the matriarch of the pod, showed no signs of physical trauma, but she was just as dead as the other four. Three of the younger whales were still living, and it was to these three that the community had already turned their attention.

Nicole was immediately assigned to work with Claude Browning on the youngest, a struggling female. Wade supervised the handling of the largest live animal, an apparently healthy male, while Dr. Thompson worked with the second surviving and much smaller male. Huge metal frames were set up with bright flood lights that shone upon the scene, making it almost as bright as daylight. Throughout the night, they worked in teams dumping seawater over the whales to keep their skin alive and digging tunnels beneath the animals to put them each into a sling. It was back-breaking work, and an assembly line was formed for each survivor. Around three in the morning, they managed to get Nicole's whale, whom she had named Baby, up into a sling. The tractor carried the two-ton infant out to the water's edge and held her aloft enough to let the waves crash around her, keeping her damp, but lifting her periodically to prevent sharks from coming after her. Nicole and Claude's team then launched a safety net out from the beach with heavy, ten-pound sinkers and floating buoys that prevented sharks from attacking their Baby.

Unfortunately, Wade's large male pilot whale died of respiratory failure before his team could secure a sling. Its massive weight crushed its lungs, preventing it from breathing. Wade redoubled his efforts with Dr. Thompson to help save the last surviving male, whom Dr. Thompson had named Joe.

By dawn, a ray of hope arrived. They might be able to save the two whales from certain expiration because a large ship, the *Luna Drifter*, had arrived with a commercial-style net.

It took until noon to transfer the two whales (now in slings) far enough into the water to use a lasso system on their tails and pull them into the looped net near the ship. Both animals were too exhausted to swim, so Nicole, Claude, Wade and Dr. Thompson went into the water with them, using the whales natural buoyancy to move them through the water, keeping them mobile. Because Nicole had seen several sharks in the area throughout the night and early that morning, she was grateful for the safety net in which Baby and Joe were held. She completely disregarded the cold of the water, her entire strength and concentration wrapped up in saving Baby.

It was well past two in the afternoon when Baby finally started swimming without assistance. Nicole and Claude were both pulled aboard the *Luna Drifter*. Nearly an hour later, Joe made similar progress, and Doctors Reilly and Thompson were hauled aboard the rescue ship.

The scientists were warmed with blankets and fed a large bowl of steaming beef broth and hot Tang. Before long, Nicole began to feel a painful tingling as circulation was restored to her blue toes and fingers. She had been so busy worrying about Baby, she had not paid attention to her own condition. Looking around at the other three of her companions, she saw that they were about as well off as herself. They had all clung to hope for the pilot whales whose lives were nearly ended. Both Joe and Baby were now being examined by two whale doctors from San Diego's Sea World, who had flown up to assist. The two animals would be returned to the wild within a few days when their strength returned.

Nicole left the group and went to the bow of the ship, where she looked through a pair of binoculars at the scene ashore. Six whales had died, and the carnage of their deaths now stretched in red streaks across the sand. A large pit was being dug inland, a half-mile north of the dark gray bodies, and tractors would soon haul the animals to the pit and bury them. Other scientists would first perform autopsies to see if they could determine a reason why the whales stranded themselves on Bullards Beach, but Nicole knew there were no definitive answers. The alpha female led her family's pod ashore to die. Fortunately, they had so far been able to save two of them, but their lives were still precariously on edge. They had a long way to go to survive in the wild ocean without their matriarch.

Tears slipped down her cheeks as Nicole contemplated the loss of the six whales, and the troubles Baby and Joe still faced. The analogy to her own life overwhelmed her. All her feelings for Charlie lay dead on the beach. The chanting in her heart that she already loved Wade Reilly continued to struggle, like Baby and Joe. She did not know if her love was strong enough to survive.

When she felt a hand upon her shoulder, she turned and found Claude Browning at her side. "Ready for a good cry over the ones we couldn't save?" he asked, blinking back a few tears of his own. She leaned into his offered shoulder and wept silently for several minutes. Claude was a dear friend, and his offer of comfort was welcome.

When she finished, she pulled back and he released her. "Thanks," she whispered. "I needed that."

"No problem," he said. "So did I."

"The dinghy's here," came Dr. Thompson's voice from the deck above them. "Ready to go ashore?"

"Sure," said Nicole, wiping her tears away with her fingers.

Claude followed her aft where they climbed down a ladder to an inflatable dinghy that took them back to Bullards Beach, two miles south of the dead whales. Their mission had been for the living, other scientists would take care of the dead.

Wade's blue eyes found hers as she sat on the gunwale and watched the shoreline grow closer. "Good job," she said to the two doctors.

"You, too," said Wade, then he turned his attention to the navigator who was piloting the dinghy back to the beach.

Nicole couldn't help but feel snubbed by Wade, but she refused to let him bother her too much. She had mourned their losses, and now she could take pleasure in their triumphs. They had saved two whales, and no one was going to dampen her spirits over that.

———•———

Wade paced back and forth in front of the motor home, his binoculars in hand. It had been five weeks since he'd met Nicole and he was sick with worry about her. Ever since the whales arrived on Bullards Beach, she had refused every opportunity to be alone with him. Whenever he showed up at her house, she would be leaving, or "not up to company," or working on her dissertation. She had also changed all the locks on the house so that his key no longer worked.

Fortunately, he still had two microphones inside the house, one on the dining room table, and one in Nicole's bedroom on her dresser, thanks to Danny's habit of giving Nicole silk flowers.

To Wade's dismay, Nicole didn't always remember to turn the security system on or lock the doors, she was still used to living carefree. Her inattention gave Wade an opportunity to tap into her security system and telephone lines. Hating himself for deceiving her, and refusing to consider whether his actions were illegal or not, he was still determined to protect her. She had no idea the danger that lurked nearby.

Wade was always relieved when he saw the red light blink on his monitoring machine, indicating Nicole had turned the security system on after she went indoors for the night. This gave Wade a small amount of peace. Like clockwork,

Nicole always telephoned Catherine Hemsley every evening at ten to tell her she was fine, staying up for the news and then she would go to bed.

Spying on Nicole did not give Wade much time for socializing or sleeping. If only he could tell Nicole the truth, but he knew she would never believe him, not without proof. And he had no proof, not yet.

However, now that Wade knew where Charlie Hackett (also known as Charlie Blaugh) had disappeared to when he left Astoria, Wade had private detectives watching his every move.

The only bright spot on the horizon was that Charlie had not come around to bother Nicole yet, as he had threatened. Their engagement was definitely over, a thing of the past, but Wade could only celebrate in silence. He, with the help of Nicole's brother, Danny, had hopefully saved Nicole from a fate worse than death; a fate Wade's sweet cousin, Sharelle, had suffered at the hands of Charlie Blaugh. Left for dead on the side of an abandoned road in western Oregon, it had taken Sharelle seven months to recover enough to go home from the hospital with her mother. Aunt Rosa had changed Sharelle's and her own last name to Smith, to hide themselves from the perpetrator. They had moved to Denver where Wade's mother had helped them start over, giving them a place where they could build a new life away from the tragedy.

The police had never conclusively proven that Sharelle had been beaten and left for dead by her ex-husband, but Wade knew otherwise. Although Charlie had an ironclad alibi from his two crewmen, Wade started an investigation of his own, but he was still coming up with dead ends. And Sharelle could not, or would not, tell the police that Charlie Hackett was the man who attacked her. Sharelle and Charlie had divorced six months before Sharelle's life was forever changed by a man who took her from her apartment in the dark of night, beat her to a bloody pulp, then threw her out of a moving car and down into a ravine, where she landed on her lower back, across a fallen tree, paralyzing her from the hips down.

For four hours, Sharelle had slowly used her swollen hands, wrists and elbows to drag her lifeless legs up that ravine and onto the road where a motorist spotted her and called the paramedics. Charlie could not be reached for an additional three days, having supposedly been on a fishing expedition aboard his boat.

Still, Wade had reason to suspect that Charlie was Sharelle's assailant. Wade deduced that Charlie had fed a batch of sleeping pills to his two crewmen, anchored his fishing vessel away from prying eyes, took his dinghy ashore, done the dirty deed, then slipped back aboard his ship and headed out to sea.

And, he doubted Nicole had seen the last of Charlie Hackett. Wade Reilly had no choice but to prepare for the worst from that man.

Unfortunately, it seemed apparent that Nicole had seen all that she wanted to see of Wade Reilly. She had avoided him at every opportunity. Cordial at work, she denied him access to her after the Institute closed for the day, claiming she was too busy, too tired, too worried about her dissertation, too irritable to give him any time alone with her. Worse, Nicole and Claude were now spending a great deal of time together after MIC hours working on her crab project.

Claude and Nicole's closeness had become apparent the day the whales were saved. They had embraced one another quite a long time aboard the *Luna Drifter*, and Wade wasn't the only one who noticed. Dr. Thompson had mentioned it a few days later. Since it was a painful topic for Wade, he had just shrugged as though he wasn't really listening. He knew Nicole and Claude were not seeing each other outside of the Institute, but Claude was staying an abnormal amount of time with Nicole after hours at the Institute.

Today, Wade had heard from Nancy Cardston that Nicole was planning to go bear hunting in two weeks with Claude Browning, Matt and Catherine Hemsley. There was no mention of Margo Browning going with them. Wade was trying to decide how could he wrangle an invite out of the Hemsleys.

Why was Nicole avoiding him so religiously?

To his utter amazement, Danny had paid him a small amount of money on the real estate contract, which was delivered through Nicole. When that first check arrived from Danny, Wade was so astounded, he worried Danny had returned to gambling, so he hired a private investigator in Denver who reported today that Danny was doing fine at the University, and would finish his last nine credit hours toward his master's degree by December fifteenth . . . with excellent grades. Wade also learned the money that he'd given Danny had been used to open a small office in a Denver suburb from which *Paraplegics Anonymous* was now operating. The check Danny had sent Wade was small, but it apparently came out of Wade's income as a part-time researcher for Schoonaker's Pharmaceuticals.

Finally able to put his concerns about Danny aside, the only thing Wade could do now was protect Nicole by waiting Charlie Hackett out, or finally proving Charlie's involvement in Sharelle's attack. Private investigators were working around the clock on both areas of concern. But that didn't mean Wade would let his guard down. Not at all.

Now, if he could just figure out how to get an invitation to a bear hunt.

———•———

Nicole's fingers felt like miniature hammers as she pounded the computer keys, writing her dissertation for her doctorate in marine biology. It seemed she had been working on this project all her life, but it had only been three short years. So close to fruition she could taste the doctorate degree in the air around her, feel it at her fingertips.

Sadly, Nicole realized there was only one thing she wanted more. And she refused herself because Wade could not measure up to the man she wanted in her future.

Two more pages. Two more and she would be finished, with only the proofreading left to do. Then, miraculously, it was one page and then the last few words appeared upon the computer screen. Immediately, she saved the six-hundred page document on several CD-Roms.

Elated, yet completely exhausted, Nicole sank off the chair and onto the floor next to the kitchen table. Never had she pushed herself so hard, mastered all other impulses, avoided all other desires. Laughing aloud, the sensation of pure joy astounding her, the last few steps toward her doctorate were exhilarating and beyond belief.

And she owed it all to Wade Reilly.

Determined to avoid Wade at all costs, Nicole had forced herself to take her degree more seriously than she had ever done before, and she had succeeded. Nicole did not want Wade Reilly to have any influence in her decisions now that she was nearing the finish line.

Recalling with vivid clarity the emotions Wade aroused so easily within her that day on the beach, she could not allow herself a repeat performance. Reluctantly, Nicole had to admit that she could not hate Wade like she wanted to, for he had somehow become a part of her reason for being. Although she did not understand her feelings, she also felt she could not trust Wade. Not at all. Something was not right about Wade's determination to pursue her, but Nicole couldn't decide with any certainty what it was, she only knew that he was not all that he seemed.

The only thing Wade had in his favor was that he had kept his promises to Nicole. He had installed a superior septic system, drilled a very deep well that bubbled with delicious water, paid for the installation of electricity and telephone service, put in an asphalt road to Grandpa's Pines, and had a large satellite system set up, enabling ready access to television and internet. Everything he had told her he would do, he had done.

She just didn't understand why he would take advantage of Danny so mercilessly. If she could just understand, maybe she could forgive him. Since she refused to see Wade outside the Institute, she had no opportunity to learn why he had outwitted Danny so readily.

Greed was the only motive that could have driven Wade to purchase her grandfather's real estate and Danny's stocks and bonds. Greed for her share, perhaps, drove him still. But sharing her property or her life with a greedy man was not how she envisioned her future.

Chapter Ten

Nicole smoothed out the edges of the comforter on her bed, snugged another sweater into her duffle bag, grabbed her rifle from over the mantle, a box of extra bullets, and headed out the door. The bear hunt in southern Oregon was an event she hoped never to miss. Her father used to take her every year. Since she turned eight years old she had participated in the hunt. After her father's demise, the Hemsleys and Claude Browning and his wife's brother, Bill, were her usual hunting companions. Except this year Bill had twisted his ankle in a fall and would not go hunting with them.

Claude held open the back door to his Buick as Nicole loaded the rest of her gear inside. Then she scooted onto the seat beside all the equipment and food she'd brought with her.

As soon as Claude had buckled his seatbelt on the passenger side up front, Margo turned the key in the ignition. "Make sure you don't let Matt do too much," warned Margo, as she put the car in gear and headed northeast toward the Coast Range Mountains. "Catherine says it's all she can do to hold him down. Stubborn as an old grizzly, he is."

"What I don't understand," said Nicole from the back seat, "is why Matt and Catherine are going up to the camp separately this year. They've never done this before."

Smiling, Margo said, "Catherine's got a surprise for someone, and that's all I'm going to say!"

Claude added, "Matt has one, too. I expect nearly getting killed seven weeks ago has made him re-evaluate his life. He was tickled as a fox with a fat squirrel last I spoke with him. Wouldn't say what he was up to, but he seemed pleased as punch about whatever it is."

"It's mighty strange," admitted Nicole, sinking back into the seat and closing her eyes, listening to Claude and Margo converse, while not really hearing what they had to say.

Of course, everything seemed odd to Nicole these days. It was already the first week of November, and she finally felt like her own life, which had been completely out of control for almost two months, was beginning to be rewarded for all her efforts, prayers and diligence.

While Wade continued lurking around her ancestral property like he owned the place, Danny was still on target with his grades and had made two payments on his real estate contract. Five more weeks to go, and Daniel would earn his master's degree in pharmaceutical research.

In addition, Nicole's crab project was finally complete, and she had Claude Browning's undying assistance to thank for it. He had been relentless in helping her in the crab lab, and she doubted she could have accomplished half as much without him. All Nicole had left to do was to finish proofreading her dissertation, then turn it in to Dr. Thompson. It would be the final step toward qualifying for her doctorate in marine biology. Dr. Thompson had already previewed some of her written work, and he said it would very likely qualify for publication. Nicole had already submitted a form for a grant that would do just that through the *University Textbook Fund*. Her understanding of the Dungeness crab, or more precisely *Cancer magister*, went well beyond the scope of any previously published study, including the one done in Louisiana on blue crabs.

Charlie Hackett had not made any effort to contact her. This time of separation had given

Nicole the opportunity to reflect on their relationship, and to realize that she had never really loved him. Because she lived such an isolated life, working forty-hour weeks at the Marine Institute in Charleston, and twenty-hour weeks in the evenings doing research on her crab lab project, then spending her summers on one marine research ship after another, diving around the globe in places that would strengthen her knowledge of sea creatures and their habitat, she had restricted the number of people with whom she would come into contact. This had severely limited the probability of finding Mr. Right. When Charlie had shown interest in her during a student fishing charter arranged through the MIC, she was flattered. But she hadn't really loved him, not like she loved Wade Reilly.

Wade had shown her that there could be fire and passion in romance, unlike any she'd ever known, and Charlie just did not thrill her with the astoundingly feverish emotion that Wade did.

Given weeks of reflection, and weeks of longing for Wade, Nicole had admitted only to herself that she was in love with him. And that thought made her angriest of all. He had no right to come into her life and disrupt it entirely. What kind of man would take advantage of a fledgling like Danny, and wield his money around like some hefty sledge hammer, purchasing Danny's stocks for half their value? What kind of man pays twenty percent on the dollar in actual real estate value, preying on someone like Danny who was vulnerable to such a predator? Although Nicole's heart, body and soul ached for Wade, her questioning mind would not allow him the opportunity to prey upon her like he had her brother. She had successfully avoided Wade at all costs simply because she could not believe that his attention had anything to do with *her*. Wade already told her he wanted to buy her half of their Oregon real estate, and she had no reason to believe that anything other than greed was his motivation for pursuing her. Nicole was too smart to fall in the same abyss into which Danny had plummeted.

Falling asleep while deep in thought came easily for Nicole. Exhausted from the rigorous schedule she had kept the past two months was taking its toll. If nothing else, she might be able to get some sleep on the bear hunt.

When the car stopped with a quick jerk, Nicole awoke. "Are we there already?" She meant the Hemsley camp, a wild piece of real estate high upon the Coast Range Mountains. Indeed, they were on a mountainside surrounded by tall pines, alders, sugar maples and Sitka spruce, in a tunnel of yellows and golds and forest green. Bare branches reached around them like arthritic fingers seeking warmth against the cold.

"It's another twenty miles," said Claude, getting out of the car. "Someone's put a log across the road."

Margo and Nicole scrambled out to help him and within a few minutes the three of them had rolled the log off to the side.

"Odd that it was here," said Margo, getting behind the steering wheel again. Claude and Nicole took their places inside the car and Margo continued driving up the ferned tunnel toward Hemsley's camp. "We had just turned onto the south fork toward Hemsley's property when that log showed up. You could tell it had been moved there deliberately."

"Yes, there were footprints in the soil around it," said Nicole. "I wonder if it has anything to do with the surprise Matt is planning."

"Are you certain you don't know what it is, Claude?" asked Margo. "After all, I know what Catherine's planning, only I'm just not saying."

"No idea," said Claude. "Anyway, I wouldn't have listened if he'd tried to tell me. Men aren't like women, dear. Nosy creatures, you are."

Margo laughed. "Like you never peek at the packages under the Christmas tree before the big day arrives."

"I only do that to make sure you haven't," he grinned.

"Okay," said Nicole from the back seat. "Change of subject. Did anyone catch the news on the tropical storm off El Salvador?"

"Terrible," said Margo. "All those people homeless like that."

Within a few minutes, Margo was busy telling Claude and Nicole about an especially interesting Judge Judy rerun she'd watched last week.

By the time they reached the camp, Matt Hemsley, who had towed his small camping trailer up the day before, was unloading firewood from the bed of his truck onto a dry tarp. To Nicole's dismay, Wade Reilly was helping him.

"Made it up, did you?" asked Matt as he opened the door for Nicole to get out. "I guess you see my surprise, Nicole. Hope you don't mind. Wade's never been on a bear hunt. Thought he could do with some local color, especially since he's leaving these parts right after Thanksgiving."

"I thought you didn't hunt game," she said to Wade as she got out of the car with her rifle in hand. "Dressed or undressed."

"Hi!" said Wade enthusiastically, ignoring her jibe. "Brought your forty-four Mauser, I see. What can I do to help?"

Nicole started unloading the car, throwing her tent at Wade first of all. She couldn't decide if she was angry he had come, or thrilled. Finally, she decided that Wade couldn't get too forward with her when she had Claude, Matt and Catherine to keep an eye on him. She would have to make the best of the situation.

"May I help you set this up?" asked Wade. "Then, perhaps you can help me set mine up? I haven't a clue how they work."

"I would have thought you had your tent up already," she teased. "Where did you sleep last night?"

"On Matt's kitchen table. It makes into a bed of sorts," he admitted. "I won't want to sleep there tonight, though. Catherine's on her way up, and the Hemsleys will need some privacy."

"I see," said Nicole, quelling her surprise and her anger for the moment.

Wade held the tent in his left arm as he shook hands with Claude and Margo. "I heard you don't usually come on the bear hunt," he said to Margo.

"Oh, I don't," she admitted. "I'll drive straight back once Catherine gets here safely."

"By yourself?" Wade asked. "Isn't that a bit dangerous?"

"I do it every year," insisted Margo. "Nothing up here but you folks and black bears. And my car is faster than any black bear, believe me."

"Besides," whispered Claude, "once she starts down the mountain, she honks the horn every ten seconds until she reaches the highway. It takes us two days to scout the bears out after that. But don't tell her it annoys us. If it comforts her, so be it."

Wade smiled. "My lips are sealed," he whispered back.

Nicole took her tent from Wade and shook it out of its protective bag. She soon had the cozy two-man tent spread out on the ground, its entrance facing the fire pit, and a nifty set of spring-bars supporting it. Then she put the rain guard over it, securing the entire assembly with metal pegs pounded into the ground with a hammer.

"Great job," he said, handing her his tent. "Don't stop on my account."

Smiling at Wade's inept abilities at camping, Nicole took his brand new tent, read the few instructions that came with it, and had his tent set up next to hers within a few minutes. When she was finished, she said to Wade. "Don't just stand there. You're at least good for packing. Haul my stuff and put it into my tent, and yours into your tent."

"That's the least I can do," he said. Following her instructions, Wade pulled her sleeping bag, pillow and ice chest out of the back of Claude's

Buick, along with two coats, her duffle bag and a spare pair of dry boots. Nicole noticed he was very careful not to let any of her gear get muddy or soiled before putting it meticulously into her tent. He was equally as cautious with his own gear, most of which was still in new boxes and sporting price tags.

By the time Wade was finished, Claude had set up his own tent on the other side of Nicole's. All three of them were facing the fire pit, which Matt had built into a roaring blaze. Matt and Catherine always slept in the small camping trailer, but the rest of the camp crew roughed it.

"Did you bring any bells?" Nicole asked Wade and Claude.

"Bells?" Wade questioned. The meek expression on his face made Nicole laugh aloud.

Claude handed her a bag full of them.

"I suppose we'll have enough. You can use a few of mine. You didn't bring string, either, did you?" she asked Wade.

"String?" he echoed.

"Don't worry, I have plenty." Nicole dug into her duffle bag and brought out a zip-loc bag full of sleigh bells, and a roll of kite string. She proceeded to string the bells in four-foot increments all around the perimeter of the camp, about six inches off the ground, using sticks for support. She did not string bells across the road.

"Hmm," said Wade. "Do they really keep the bears away?"

"No," she laughed teasingly. "But they make a great alarm system should any bears happen to wander into our camp at night."

They were adjusting a few bells on the far side of Wade's tent when Nicole heard the honking of a car. She looked up to see Catherine's van pulling into the campsite. After Catherine parked the van, Nicole stood up and started toward her door, but stopped the moment she saw him. Catherine's surprise was, apparently, for Nicole. She had brought Charlie Hackett with her.

"Surprise!" Catherine exclaimed as she got out of the van and gave Nicole a big hug, whispering, "You won't believe who I brought with me, Nicole, so be a good girl and give him a hearty welcome."

Nicole was certainly shocked, if not downright flabbergasted.

"Hi, Nicole," said Charlie, getting out of the passenger door. "Guess Catherine's gonna' play matchmaker for us."

"How kind of her," came Wade's growl from behind the tent. He stood up and glared at Charlie.

Catherine stopped in her tracks. "Why, Dr. Reilly, whatever– "

"Wade was my surprise," said Matt. "Guess we should have communicated a little better, wife. I thought your surprise was a new hunting dog for me."

Catherine frowned ominously. "And I thought you had bought me that new camping trailer I wanted," she accused. "I don't know what gets into that head of yours, Matt Hemsley. Honestly!"

"Why don't we help Charlie get settled in?" suggested Nicole. "Wade, you can help carry Catherine's groceries into the trailer for her."

"Naw, I should go back," said Charlie. "You're not staying, are you, Mrs. Browning?"

"No, but– " Margo began.

"No reason Nicole can't have two suitors vying for her attention," said Claude. "A little competition will probably do you both good."

"I'm staying," Wade said, though it sounded more like a challenge. He stroked the keypad of his satellite telephone which hung from his belt.

Charlie gave him a dangerous scowl and said stubbornly, "Me, too." His hand went automatically to the knife in its sheath, hanging from his own belt.

"Great!" said Matt. "Won't this be fun!"

Afterward, Claude kissed Margo goodbye and watched until she had driven completely out of sight, then he helped Wade carry groceries to the trailer for Catherine.

Meanwhile, Nicole helped Charlie get his tent set up and his gear loaded inside it. "I didn't mean to cause a fuss," said Charlie. "I told Mrs. Hemsley you wouldn't want me here."

"I'm glad you came, Charlie," said Nicole. "We parted on poor terms and I don't think either of us wanted that."

"No, we didn't," Charlie admitted. "I haven't stopped thinking about you, Nicole. Not for one minute. I'm sorry I got so angry, but when you kissed Dr. Reilly, I went into a rage."

"I understand," she said. "Let's just forget about it, shall we?"

"You're still seeing him?" Charlie asked as he pounded a stake into the ground.

"It's hard not to, he works out at MIC, and he lives in a motor home up at Grandpa's Pines." Nicole handed him another stake, which he drilled into the soft ground.

"Are you dating him?" Charlie asked, and she could hear the anger in his voice.

"I'm dating no one," she admitted. "I've been working too hard on my dissertation and preparing my oral thesis. That and the crab project has taken up all my time."

"Would you like to go out with me some-time?" he asked, but it sounded more like a challenge than an entreatment.

"No," Nicole shook her head. "I've had a lot of time to think about us, Charlie. I don't think we were such a great idea. I'd still like to consider you a friend, though."

"It's all or nothin' with me, Babe," he growled softly. "I ain't gonna be available to dangle on a string."

"I'm sorry you feel that you were dangled at all," she said, refusing to give him the last stake. In his anguished state, he didn't need a weapon.

Charlie stood up and glared menacingly. Nicole watched his eyes as the fire in them was cloaked effectively. He held out his hand for the last stake. "Sorry," he said. "I shouldn't 'a said that. We should be able to act like adults about this, I guess." He gave her a determined smile.

Sensing no more threat from him, Nicole handed him the stake, which he pounded into the ground without further comment. "Thank you, Charlie. I appreciate that."

He grunted softly, but otherwise did not respond.

By the time evening settled on the camp, Charlie was telling fish tales and Matt was matching them blow by blow with bear tales of his own.

Catherine Hemsley ran a very organized camp, and had posted a chart with chores listed upon it on a kitchen station she had set up at one of three tables. Wade and Nicole had the first night's dishes. Meanwhile, Charlie and Claude had firewood duty, and Catherine was helping Matt put away all the food they didn't eat that night.

"Great supper," Wade said conversationally.

"A little heavier than I like," she admitted. "But Catherine loves to cook, and I only go on the hunt once a year."

"How long have you been coming up here?" he asked, drying a tin cup.

"This is my twenty-first year," she said. "My dad used to bring us up when we were kids." Nicole put the last pan into the dishwater and started scrubbing it.

"You must love it," he observed. "Camping seems to bring out the color in your face."

"I do. I mean, it does?"

"Yes, but I notice you always swish your hand around the basin before you put in any-more dishes." His smile caught Nicole off guard.

"Automatic reflex," she confessed. "When I was fifteen and on one of these camping trips, my brother put a big frog in my dishwater when I wasn't looking. The nasty thing jumped out at me and landed on my chest. I screamed and threw the pan I was holding at Danny. Missed him, thank goodness. My dad used to say that frog scared me so bad my growth halted right then and there. I never grew any taller after that."

"And you never figured out that, at fifteen, you'd likely reached your maximum height?" he laughed.

"Of course, but I loved the way Dad always told the story afterward."

"Nicole, that day on the beach, I– " he began unexpectedly.

"Don't," she insisted. "Don't say anything. That day on the beach meant nothing to me."

"You're sure?" he asked. "Because I could have sworn you felt something."

"I did," she agreed. "But I quashed it, and you should, too. We're not compatible, Wade. I may enjoy your touch, but what you've done gets in my way and I can't let that go."

"The truth is not always what it seems," he whispered, taking her hand from the dishwater and placing it against his chest. "I think we can be a very good match."

Nicole felt herself tremble inside. She could easily be persuaded to rekindle the Oregon flame within her. It took every ounce of strength and determination she had not to throw herself recklessly into his arms. Refusing the feelings he ignited, she said, "No, Wade. We can't. Please, just let it go at that."

"Why won't you trust me?" he questioned, releasing her hand. "Didn't Danny ask you to trust me? You should see the situation from my eyes." He nodded toward Charlie Hackett. "And I'm not the one you shouldn't trust."

"Aren't you?" she asked, her voice sharp, calculating. "You're the one who took advantage of my brother. I still haven't figured out why, Wade. You must have all the money you need. Until I can understand how you could use my brother the way you have, the only conclusion I can make about you is that you're callously greedy. And that's one side of you I cannot tolerate."

Chapter Eleven

Claude, Matt and Charlie entertained the camp with their competitive stories until late that night, while Charlene and Nicole strung another batch of bells across the road leading into the camp. Wade had been quiet and withdrawn the rest of the evening, but Nicole noticed him watching her several times. He seemed shameless at hiding his interest in her. Charlie had glared at him a couple of times, but at those moments, Claude, ever alert to any problem that may arise, eased the tension with a tale from the vast knowledge in his marine-biology-saturated mind.

It was nearing midnight before Nicole climbed into her tent only to toss and turn, remembering the night's events. Knowing she had spoken harshly to Wade, finally confessing to him the battle that raged within her, made Nicole feel more vulnerable rather than the opposite. For some reason, she just could not let the matter go, regardless how hard she tried. Wade wanted her to trust him, but how could she? Granted, he'd done everything he told her he would do, and that earned high marks in her score board. But manipulating Danny into selling everything to Wade at prices far below rock-bottom value was beyond her comprehension. His purchases did not seem to fit his character, and until she could understand why he'd done it, she could not begin to forgive him.

By two in the morning, unable to sleep, Nicole crawled out of the tent, added wood to the dying embers of the campfire, filled a pot with water and hung it over the fire pit to let it heat. She was planning to make some hot chocolate, hoping it would help her sleep.

As she sat on a log near the fire, she heard some indefinable noise just north of the camp, coming from behind a tall redwood. Cautiously, she removed her forty-four Mauser from her tent and headed in the direction of the sound, being extra careful not to make any noise herself, and stepping over the string with the bells on it that she had strung earlier. The damp mist that hung in the air like a dense cloak made her footsteps inaudible. Her main problem was the poor visibility. The dense fog hid everything ten feet away from her view.

Drawing nearer the tree in the darkness, she recognized Wade's voice, but it was a one-sided conversation. "I've already alerted them to our presence," he said, his voice a near whisper. "No, Dan. Just keep our position handy, in case I call you. If there is an emergency, your directions will hasten the speed with which the sheriff and his deputies can proceed. They won't be able to trace a 9-1-1 call from a satellite phone, but with your knowledge of this place, you will know the fastest route and how to direct them. "

A long pause hesitated Nicole's movement. Why was Wade talking to Danny this early in the morning, and what sort of emergency was he expecting that would necessitate the sheriff being called? She decided it was time to make her presence known. Quickly, she kicked a rock that went skidding forward, thumping into the redwood. "Shh," she heard Wade warn. "Someone's up." The sound of a button on Wade's satellite phone being pressed reached her ears next, and she knew that Wade had disconnected the call.

"How many men named Dan do you know, Wade?" she asked quietly, not wanting to awaken the rest of the camp. Nicole stepped out from her side of the tree to face Wade Reilly, her rifle held limp in her hand.

"Only one," he answered, hooking the satellite phone onto his belt. The grim set of Wade's jaw told her that whatever it was, he was very serious about it. "And put that gun down before you shoot someone."

Nicole put the safety on her rifle and leaned it against the tree. "What are you up to now?"

"Sorry," Wade apologized. "Should I not have hung up? Did you want to speak to your brother?"

"You're evading my question," she accused. "What's going on?"

"How much of my conversation did you hear?" he asked. "I'll need to know what you missed before I can tell you anything."

"You've got Danny standing by for a call from you, so he can notify the sheriff to come up here, for starters. Why?" Nicole did not understand.

"It's complicated," he began, "and I don't think we'll have time to discuss everything right now."

"Why not?" she demanded. "I want to know what you and my brother are up to this time." When she heard a bear bell's tinkling on the still night air, she realized they were not alone.

"Charlie's headed our way," said Wade. "This isn't a good time to explain."

"But you will explain . . . as soon as possible?" she questioned.

Wade nodded. "I will, if you'll promise me one thing. Don't let Charlie get you alone for a second, Nicole. I don't trust him."

Trying to process what Wade was trying to tell her, and having seen Charlie's temper flare thrice already, she nodded and changed the subject. "Why come on a bear hunt, Dr. Reilly, if you don't shoot game?" she asked, trying to keep her voice steady.

"I figured it's the only way I'll get a chance to spend any time with you."

"So you two ain't still seeing each other?" Charlie interrupted.

"No, we're not," insisted Nicole. "Dr. Reilly is merely a land tenant at the moment, and didn't I hear Matt say something about your leaving come Thanksgiving?" Her question was directed to Wade.

"Perhaps," Wade answered evasively.

"So why did you say you came on the hunt?" asked Charlie.

"Like you, Mr. Hackett, is it? I wanted to spend more time with Nicole." Wade challenged.

"I've been trying to place you ever since you arrived at Nicole's place," said Charlie. "And I think I finally have you figured out. It took me a while before I remembered. But Reilly was my ex-wife's aunt's name. Teresa Reilly. You're related to my ex-wife, Sharelle, aren't you?"

Wade nodded as his eyes narrowed in a glaring manner. "She's my cousin."

"Hmmpf! I thought so. Shame what happened to her," Charlie nearly choked on his words, but Nicole couldn't tell whether it was from sorrow or disgust. His next sentence answered that concern. "She'd have been better off if she'd died that night. Lucky for me, I was at sea while it happened."

"You told me Sharelle left you for another man," said Nicole, surprised to hear this much about Sharelle. Had Wade been correct in warning her that Charlie was not the one she should trust?

"She did, Babe," said Charlie smoothly, stepping forward and taking Nicole's hand in his. When he spoke again, he sounded almost as though he had rehearsed the story over and over again: "Six months later, someone beat her to a bloody pulp and threw her into a ravine up by the Columbia River Gorge area. She was paralyzed from the waist down. I expect her boyfriend was involved in it, but he had an airtight alibi. Some other dame was sleeping with him that night."

Wade glared Charlie down and his voice crackled with emotion. "Sharelle left you because after you spent all her inheritance she had the nerve to complain, so you beat her up several times. She was too ashamed to tell anyone you were abusing her, or how you'd cheated her out of half a million dollars. Her only recourse was to divorce you."

"That's a lie!" challenged Charlie. "Sharelle gave me that money of her own free will."

"Sharelle says otherwise," Wade insisted. "She also says that it was you who tried to kill her six months later. You're the man who threw her into that ravine, thinking she was dead. But she refused to give up, Charlie. She asked me to find you, to make you pay for what you did to her," Wade hissed.

"A pack of lies," snapped Charlie, squeezing Nicole's hand fiercely.

"Stop," Nicole said, trying to pull her hand free. "You're hurting me, Charlie."

"Not as bad as I'm gonna'!" Charlie insisted, removing his knife from its sheath with his other hand.

"Charlie, tell me the truth about Sharelle," Nicole tried next, hoping her fingers would not break under the pressure of his closed fist around them.

"It's been four years since Sharelle was hurt," said Charlie and his voice sounded desperately calm. "Four years and the cops haven't arrested me, Nicole. If I was guilty, I would be locked up in jail right now."

Wade clarified Charlie's response. "Your two crewmen still swear they were with you that night, on a fishing trip out at sea. Only you slipped them something to make them sleep, didn't you?" Wade asked. "You anchored the trawler, took the dinghy back into Astoria, beat Sharelle mercilessly, threw her down the ravine, then motored the dinghy back out to your boat. By the time your crew woke up, you were out to sea, and they never knew anything else happened."

"But Charlie," Nicole gasped. "You've never had any crewmen that I know about. I thought only your two brothers worked with you."

"Shut up, Nicole! You don't know anything about me or my brothers."

"But you told me once. You said you always fished alone."

"Shut up!" Charlie roared. His movements were so swift, she had no time to react. One moment he was yelling at her, the next instant he had his left hand over her throat and his knife pointed menacingly at Wade.

Nicole struggled to remove his hand from her neck, but he brought the knife up against her throat, then whipped his other hand up to her hair, yanking her head backward.

"Go for that phone and she's dead," he warned Wade. "Get your hands up where I can watch them."

As Wade lifted his hands into the air, Charlie pressed the blade against her throat and hissed, "It'll be so easy, Nicole. After Sharelle, I learned not to leave no witnesses behind. But you're wrong," he said to Wade. "My crewmen were my brothers. They helped me do Sharelle. We took care of her aboard my boat before we left the dock. As soon as it was dark we took her body up and dumped it in that ravine. You see, bodies don't wash ashore in the forest. They wouldn't have found her for years, if she hadn't been so stubborn. By then, the mountain lions and bobcats would have scattered her bones far and wide."

"So your crewmen were your brothers, and as easily as you change your name, they've changed theirs. The police would never know you were brothers."

"Nicole's the only one who knew that . . . until now. And neither of you are going to live long enough to tell a soul."

Any fear or anger Nicole felt, she quashed immediately. If she and Wade were to survive

Charlie's brutality, it would take cunning and manipulation.

"Charlie, think about what you're doing," she pleaded, surprised that her voice sounded so calm when inside she was screaming. "Put the knife down, Charlie. You don't want to hurt anyone."

"Only you, Babe. And him!" he hissed loud enough to wake the entire camp. "Do you know how long I worked, how relentlessly I pursued you?"

Grasping at any thought that entered her mind, Nicole gasped, "Because you love me, right? That doesn't have to change. Charlie, it doesn't have to end like this. I–"

"Yes, it does, Nicole. Thanks to Reilly here, you no longer have all the assets you had when we first started dating. Of course, I had planned to kill Danny right after we got married, that way you'd own all his stocks and real estate, and then you were going to have a little accident off that cliff at that place you call Grandpa's Pines, where you like to sit and watch the waves and the whales. It would have worked, if not for your man, Reilly. The police would have thought you committed suicide, after all, you would be distraught over your brother's death, and you wouldn't be able to cope with the loss of one more family member. That would have left everything to me. But Reilly had other plans. I was able to keep below his radar for over three years, but somehow he found me, probably through your no-account brother. Then, he conned Danny out of everything." The disgust was evident in Charlie's voice. He hated Wade Reilly and he did not try to hide it.

Charlie continued, "Word on the street is Danny won't let you pay off his debts. So I've been cheated out of real estate, but I can still have your stocks and bonds. I learned how to forge your signature. And at that break-in a while back, Bo and Devin stole Catherine Hemsley's Notary Public stamp, among other things. At least we'll have that much to brag about when the boys and I head up to Canada for a while."

"Charlie, killing us doesn't make any sense. There are still three people back in camp."

"It makes plenty of sense, Nicole. By now, my brothers should be just beyond the camp boundaries, waiting for my signal to come in and help. I think we can handle three age-challenged idiots, especially after you two are no longer any threat. No one expects you all back in Bandon for a week. By the time you're missed, we'll be out of the country."

Wade laughed bitterly, "You don't think I hadn't planned for this, Charlie Hackett? Or should I call you Charlie Blaugh. That was your name when you married my cousin. Before that it was Chuck Jones, wasn't it? That sweet young thing in Eugene, Oregon. Callie Hilton? Her rich daddy died in a car accident two weeks before you married her. They never found her body. What did you do with Callie Hilton?"

Charlie glared ominously. "She's dead as you'll be in a minute. Hid her in Brubaker's truck, underneath one of his bear skins. Then, I conned him into bringing me back to his place. We got drunk as skunks that night, but by morning, I'd hauled her body off and buried her. Near as Brubaker knew, my alibi was firm and so was his. Besides, I was going by Charlie Blaugh by then, and no one else knew me as Chuck Jones."

"But why, Charlie?" Nicole asked, hoping to keep Charlie talking. "Why did you kill Callie?"

"Her daddy's money started to mysteriously disappear and she blamed me for it, can you imagine?" he taunted. "Like Sharelle, Callie decided to take what little she had left and leave me behind. But no one walks out on me, Nicole, not even you!"

Nicole watched in horror as Charlie lifted up his hand, the knife blade black and ominous in the mist around them. At that moment, she knew Charlie intended to kill her. She screamed, but an instant before the knife could be thrust in her chest, Charlie was thrown sideways. Wade crashed into him with one sudden burst of energy. The knife went sailing off into the air as the two men collided. Wade's satellite telephone dislodged and fell to the ground where the two men scuffled, Wade getting a few good swings at Charlie's face before Charlie grabbed a rock and hit Wade on the side of the head.

During their struggle, Nicole grabbed the Mauser from beside the tree and shot a warning blast into the air that shocked both men into silence. "That's enough!" she said. "Tie him up, Wade. Then call the sheriff."

"I ain't leavin' without what I came for," Charlie growled and lunged toward her, his attention diverted from Wade by the blast.

Surprisingly, Claude used that moment to pounce on Charlie from behind a tree and, with Wade's assistance, wrapped Charlie's wrists together with duct tape.

"Claude!" Nicole gasped. "How did you know?"

"Wade warned me," said Claude. "I've been taping the whole conversation."

"Warned me, too," said Matt, hobbling up the hill toward them. "Your shot woke me up, Nicole. And if Charlie's brothers are around, they heard it, too. Perhaps we have a bargaining chip by keeping Charlie immobile and in plain view."

The three men wrapped Charlie's legs and feet together with duct tape, then carried him down to camp where they sat him on an old tree stump by the fire, Matt and Claude standing guard, their guns cocked and ready in their arms.

By the time Wade remembered his satellite telephone, retrieved it and called the sheriff's office, Charlie was subdued, his ankles taped to the "seat" upon which he was sitting. Charlie's foul mouth had been taped shut, as well, to prevent a stream of profanities from disturbing the others. Twice Charlie had called his brothers' names, Bo and Devin. The two brothers had not yet responded, and may not show at all once the sheriff and his deputies arrived. But they were no doubt nearby, perhaps making sure Charlie would not be harmed.

In the meantime, all eyes and ears at camp were at attention, waiting for any sound or sight through the dark misty night. The brothers would have to get past the bear bells before they could see anyone in the camp due to the heavy mist in the dark night. Visibility was only about ten to twelve feet, except immediately around the campfire.

Chapter Twelve

After discussing several strategies in whispers while guarding Charlie, they finally decided most of them would hide in plain sight around the small campfire, their eyes surveying the camp's perimeter. This way, they would have full visual range of any movement beyond them, and the two men could not sneak up on them for a surprise attack. Since Bo and Devin had not yet arrived, it seemed evident that they had not completed the twenty-mile hike up the mountain from the fork in the road. Without powerful fog lights such as the sheriff's car had, it would be suicide to drive up here in the dense mist, so they waited quietly, whispering when they felt it necessary to talk. Claude Browning braved a walk around the camp's perimeter, inside the many bells they had strung out, using a flashlight to survey the area. But, even with that light trained on the group huddled around the dying embers of the campfire, the fog was too thick to make anyone out. Charlie's brothers would have to proceed at least thirty feet beyond the bells in order to see well enough to shoot anyone.

Catherine instructed Wade to sit down on a campstool while she tended to Wade's head where a large bump had appeared, spotted with blood and a deep bruise.

Nicole set her rifle down and picked up an ice pack. She was trembling so much she could hardly hold the ice pack still against Wade's head, and he finally pulled her down onto his lap and held her comfortingly while she shivered, and let Catherine press the ice against his wound. Catherine hovered around them like a mother hen, saying, "I'm so sorry, Nicole. This was all my fault. I should have known something was up when Charlie asked me to bring him on the hunt this year. But he said he just wanted a chance to make up. I'm so sorry."

"You didn't know," Wade soothed. "I should have insisted Matt tell you, but he didn't want you to worry needlessly."

Trembling still, while Catherine had made a big pot of chamomile tea and insisted everyone drink some of it, Nicole did not know how to express to Wade how grateful she was that he had saved her life. Instinctively, Nicole knew Charlie intended to kill her when he told her no-body walks away from him. She'd known for only a split second, but Wade had anticipated Charlie's attack. He had been ready to stop Charlie at whatever cost to himself. How do you thank someone for heroics like that? Words of gratitude from Nicole could not possibly express how she truly felt.

Nicole, curled up on Wade's lap, loved the comfort of his arms around her, and stayed far longer than she should have. It took nearly an hour and a healthy portion of Catherine's tea before Nicole's shivering finally stopped. The group stayed huddled around the campfire to-gether and talked in hushed whispers, waiting for Charlie's brothers to arrive. No one doubted the two criminals would make some attempt to overpower them and rescue their brother. Charlie sat dangerously near them, but they had put one of Matt's heavy jackets and an old hat on him. Unless Bo and Devin were within ten feet of Charlie's face, they would not recognize him.

Ever alert to the sounds of the forest, they whispered their concerns about Bo and Devin, and their eventual appearance. Nicole could only hope the two brothers would show up after the police did. It was going to be a long wait. The nearest sheriff's department was at least ninety minutes away, and with the thick fog that night, it could be longer.

"Dr. Reilly," said Catherine. "What made you suspect Charlie Hackett would do something like this?" Catherine had never been given prior knowledge to Wade's suspicions.

Wade brushed Nicole's hair away from his face, for she still wanted nothing more than to have him hold her, and said, "He nearly killed my cousin, Sharelle, over four years ago. When I found out it was him, and went after him, he'd disappeared from the Astoria area. I searched everywhere, had detectives looking for him, but he'd changed his name, and the name of his boats. He's been at this kind of game for at least fifteen years, always one step ahead of the law."

"You think he intended to kill all of us up here?" Catherine persisted.

"I think he's capable of killing anyone, and doesn't seem to have much remorse over the ones he's already murdered."

Nicole heard the bitterness in Wade's voice, and felt his anger and regret that he'd not been able to track Charlie down any sooner. "But you've stopped him now, Wade," she soothed, stroking his face with her gloved hand. "The police will be here soon, and this will all be over. You're a hero."

"No," he scolded. "Not until Bo and Devin are captured, too."

Claude made a startled leap from his position by the fire. "That's it!" he exclaimed. "I think I've finally figured out what that log was all about."

His words sharpened Nicole's reflexes and quickened her mind. "The one across the road?" Nicole asked, reluctantly pulling herself away from Wade's lap and sitting on a campstool beside Claude Browning.

Claude sat back down and nodded. "Catherine said Charlie asked her just this morning . . . well, yesterday morning now . . . if he could come on the bear hunt. I'm betting he followed you up the day before, Matt, but from a distance. He apparently didn't see which fork you took to get up here. Your camp is on the south fork of the river, while the north fork goes on up to Brubaker's place."

"Of course!" agreed Nicole. " I'll bet Charlie put that log in the road, knowing it would be moved out of the way if our camp was on the south fork. That way, he'd be able to find us up here if Catherine told him no, that she wouldn't bring him."

Charlie glared at them angrily, a muffled retort could not escape his duct tape. He was positioned so that he couldn't see any of the forest but up the mountain, and his brothers would certainly come from behind him, which gave him less chance of spotting them and sending some sort of eye signal to them, should they happen to overstep the bear bells.

Claude agreed heartily. "If the log was undisturbed, Charlie and his brothers would deduce that we were on the north fork of the river."

"I thought that was Brubaker's place," observed Wade.

"Hadn't Charlie already been to Brubaker's place before?" Nicole asked.

"That's right," Wade responded, apparently wondering about the same thing.

"But," inserted Claude, "Charlie said he and Brubaker had been drinking when he buried the Hilton girl up in these mountains. It's conceivable Charlie could not remember which fork to take."

"Then what's to stop Brubaker from moving the log, if it had been on his road?" asked Wade.

Catherine jumped into the conversation. "Brubaker only goes to town the third day of the month when his Social Security check comes. He does his marketing, then goes back up to his cabin. Everyone knows that, even the fishermen."

Matt agreed. "Old Brubaker made his trip into town last Monday. He's not going back down again until December third."

They were silent for a moment, contemplating this information, when Nicole thought she heard a footstep in the forest. Matt apparently heard it, too. Standing up, Matt whispered, "Showtime. I'll be in the trailer as planned. Be careful, Catherine," he said, giving his wife a quick kiss on the cheek. Then, he headed into the trailer with his hunting rifle and closed the door quietly.

It was still so dark and misty, it would be difficult to tell if anyone left the campfire circle. But Matt's absence brought the intense anticipation in the group to an ominous level.

"Who would have thought those rumors about Charlie Hackett were true?" asked Catherine. She had insisted she stay outdoors because she could outdraw anyone with the pistol in her holster. "I never dreamed. I thought it was all hogwash."

"It wasn't," Wade responded. "But if we're careful, and God smiles upon us now, it'll all be over soon . . . for all three brothers."

Nicole leaned against him from her campstool and stared deep into his eyes. She saw the conflict within them as Wade attempted to share the truth with her, with all of them.

"Sharelle is really your cousin," she whispered. It was more statement than a question.

"She goes by Sharelle Smith these days," admitted Wade. "Her mother and mine are sisters."

"Sharelle Whitney?" asked Catherine. "She's that woman who was beaten and left for dead near Astoria a few years ago?"

"The same," nodded Wade. "She married Charlie Hackett four years ago, back when he was going by the surname Blaugh. She divorced him eight months later. Six months after that, she was beaten up and tossed into a ravine. The police could never prove it was her ex-husband, Charlie, but they haven't ruled him out completely, either. His alibi is the word of two seamen, supposed crew aboard his ship."

"Charlie never took crew with him," said Nicole. "He's always captained alone. His two brothers, Bo and Devin, captain his other two boats."

"Then they were the two who gave Charlie such an ironclad alibi?" asked Catherine.

One of the bear bells jingled, and Nicole turned her head toward the sound. All four of them stood in unison, facing the tinkling sound, still unable to see anyone approaching.

"Under false names," agreed Wade.

"But they did more than give Charlie an alibi," Nicole said, cocking her rifle. "Those two helped Charlie attack Sharelle. They're just as guilty as he is."

"That may be, little lady," came a gruff voice Nicole recognized as Bo Hackett. "But we're also the two that are gonna' finish the job Charlie came for tonight!" Bo's challenging words came out of the mist about the same time as their two husky, round-headed bodies sharpened out of the fog. They, too, had rifles pointed straight at the four gathered around the camp. "You see, we try not to leave any witnesses behind."

Wade, Claude and Nicole were standing ready, their own rifles pointed back at the intruders. Catherine held her Glock forty steadily aimed at Bo's heart.

"This one's gonna' be tough, Charlie," said Bo, the older of the three brothers. "I'm gettin' tired of cleanin' up after you."

"You're outnumbered," warned Wade. "You shoot us, they shoot you and I shoot your brother." He stepped aside to let Bo and Devin look at Charlie, bound tenaciously to a tree stump. Wade pointed his rifle directly at Charlie's temple.

"Wrong," said Bo, cocking his rifle and pointing the weapon directly at Nicole's forehead.

Devin followed his lead. "See, we don't care all that much about Charlie. He's been nothin' but trouble since the day he was born. You can go ahead and kill him, if you'd like."

Charlie squirmed in his bindings, but he was bound so thoroughly he could not respond as he may have wanted.

Bo continued, "But we figure, sure, you might kill one of us. Maybe both of us. But whichever one us you don't kill first is gonna' kill Nicole, and that's a fact." He spit a wad of chewing tobacco on the ground at Nicole's feet.

Nicole cringed in horror as she saw both Wade and Claude exchange worried glances as they seemed to consider the alternatives. After a moment's hesitation, they seemed to agree it would be best to lower their rifles. Catherine, on the other hand, steadied her aim. With lightning speed, before she had a chance to squeeze the trigger, Bo changed positions long enough to shoot Catherine in the right shoulder. Catherine screamed, dropped her gun and sank upon the ground, but she bled very little. Nicole didn't know if the wound was serious or not.

Claude looked as though he was going to go to her, but Bo had his sights back on Nicole's head again. "Leave her," he growled, kicking her revolver out of the way. Claude straightened.

"Toss your weapons over there," he said, nodding to where the revolver lay, hilt buried beneath damp orange and yellow leaves.

Claude was first to respond. He clicked on the safety and tossed his rifle aside. Wade held his ground until he looked in Nicole's eyes. Apparently, he recognized that she was not going to back down. He nodded slightly to her, indicating that she should follow his example. Then, Wade tossed his weapon aside.

Now it was only Nicole who had a weapon against two men with rifles aimed right at her head. She couldn't back down, she wouldn't. Someone had to stand up to these men, and she didn't consider her life as valuable as Claude and Wade apparently did. Feeling panicked, Nicole wondered what she should do.

Wade tried to distract them by saying, "You boys are fools if you think you can get away with this. You'll slip up. You let Sharelle live, and that was your first mistake."

"Naw," said Devin with a wicked chuckle. "Sharelle's too terrified to say anything."

"Like I said," Wade inserted, apparently trying to keep the attention on himself, "your careful planning failed. You left Sharelle alive, and its only a matter of time before she tells us that you helped Charlie beat her up."

"We can slit her throat anytime we want," said Devin. "She ain't no threat, not anymore."

"Chick's too scared to say who did it, isn't she?" asked Bo in an angry, menacing tone, keeping his sights on Nicole. "Changed her name to Smith. Lives in Denver, now. Can't get out of her wheelchair by herself. We pay her a visit every now and then at that clinic where she works. She's never gonna' talk."

The callous tone he used made Nicole realize that to this man, Sharelle was just a piece of human garbage. Their only hope for a rescue was from the sheriff's men now, so Nicole stepped forward and dared Bo with, "Surely you know that you'll never get away with killing the four of us!"

"Shut your mouth!" Bo screeched. "Or you'll be the first to die."

"Sharelle already talked to me," Wade bluffed. "Otherwise, why am I here? Why do I have documented evidence of your activities over the last three years? You think I don't know who's been terrorizing Bandon, breaking into houses, stealing and plundering?"

"You've got nothin'," barked Bo. "Devin, start with the old woman first, and keep it quiet. We don't want that Brubaker nosing around."

Devin let his rifle down, removed a switchblade knife from his jacket pocket and opened it menacingly.

Just then, Nicole heard her father's voice, whispering in her ear, *Hit the dirt, Niki. This is not your fight.* Through the fog, she thought she saw a glint of metal from the trailer window, and realized that Matt had his rifle aimed at Bo, but Claude was in his line of fire. Again, her father's voice whispered in her ear, *Don't you worry about Claude, Niki. Hit the dirt. NOW!*

For only a fraction of a section she saw Matt nod his head, as though that were his signal. He was going to fire.

Nicole's eyes widened in alarm and she yelled as she threw herself onto the ground, "DOWN!"

Catherine screamed. A flash of fire leapt through the window just as Claude flew toward the ground, his arms over his head, his body landing with a resounding thump, as though someone had tackled him there.

The rifle Bo held pointed skyward and went off as Bo was shot through the chest and knocked onto his back by the blast. Blood seeped from his chest, and his eyes flickered for only a moment, then he went lifeless.

The blast startled Devin long enough for Wade to get in one good swing to his jaw. Devin went down, but he retained his rifle and knife. Wade kicked the rifle out of Devin's hand and wrestled him for the knife. Matt came roaring out of the trailer like a mad lion, his rifle in his hand. As Wade struggled with Devin on the ground right next to the fire, Matt tripped and fell forward. The barrel of his rifle miraculously struck the pot of boiling tea that dangled over the fire pit.

The scalding tea spilled all over Devin's left thigh. Devin dropped his knife and screamed out in pain, "AAAARGH! Get it off me! Get it off!"

Wade unzipped the man's pants and pulled them off him. The skin on Devin's left leg was already blistered and inflamed. He lifted him up onto one of the camp tables.

Meanwhile Claude removed the switchblade before Devin's outstretched hand could reach it. Matt stood up and gathered all the rifles, securing them safely near the trailer, then he grabbed a towel and went to his wife, where he put pressure upon her bullet hole.

Devin yelled, agonizing over the pain from his wicked burn.

"It's just a flesh wound, dear," Catherine insisted, getting up quickly. "And this poor man needs cool water." Ignoring her shoulder, Catherine headed for the trailer. Within a few moments she brought a roasting pan full of cool water, which she started pouring over Devin's leg to ease his pain.

"These are the guys who robbed me!" Matt declared, when he finally realized his wife would not be pampered when there was someone else whom she considered in greater need than herself.

Devin grimaced. "I ain't sayin' nothin' 'til I see a lawyer." As the pain from his burn eased, he turned and looked over at the dead body of his brother, Bo. Realization hit him right where it hurts. "You killed my brother?" He lunged toward Matt, but Wade held him back. "You killed my brother, you– "

Claude placed a strip of duct tape over his mouth. "That's enough of that," Claude said. "It looks to me like the biggest mistake you ever made was leaving Matt alive the night you robbed his house." Then, to make sure Devin wouldn't try anything more, Claude taped Devin's wrists to two of the camp table legs.

Tears of anguish slipped down Devin's face, dripping across the duct tape and around his ears. Nicole noticed that no one felt remotely sorry for Devin's loss. Charlie, however, was wailing beneath his taped mouth.

Wade stayed busy bringing more water to Catherine, to help her ease the pain of Devin's burns. Nicole wanted him to stop, wanted him to hold her, to comfort her, but even she could not deny that Devin's needs came first, regardless how much suffering he had put others through.

She sank upon a camp chair next to where Claude was sitting, his hands trembling much like she had done earlier after they had subdued Charlie.

"It's over," she soothed, reaching out to hold his hands steady.

"It was your father," Claude said. "He saved my life. He told me to hit the dirt, just like he told you, but I froze. So he tackled me just like they do in a football game."

"You heard Dad tell me to– "

Matt apparently overheard them, because he came over to Nicole and squatted down eye level with her, putting his hands upon her shoulders. Choking back tears, he said, "Your Dad *was* here this morning, Nicole. I watched him say something to you and Claude. When you threw yourself down, I watched your dad push Claude to the ground. At the same moment, he yelled to me to pull the trigger."

Nicole felt the moisture spill from her eyes and slip down her face. "Now, I know," she said, unable to hold her emotions back. "Now I have proof that Dad's really out there, watching over me. You two are my living proof." She smiled gratefully through her tears.

———●———

When the police finally brought Nicole and Wade back to Bandon-by-the-Sea, she asked him to please come into the house with her for a little while. Nicole wasn't ready to face her house alone, and Wade had been extraordinarily comforting to her ever since the police arrived and took the three brothers away. They had just lived through a terrible nightmare together, starting with Charlie's arrival at Hemsley's camp.

After making them both a cup of hot chocolate, Nicole sank onto the sofa and curled up against Wade to drink it. He did not protest the position, but put his arm around her and held her silently, long enough for both of them to finish the chocolate. Nicole removed the cups to the kitchen, then returned to the sofa, tucked her feet beneath her and leaned against Wade once again, where he held her close for several long minutes.

Finally, Nicole said, "I want you to start at the beginning, Wade."

"You heard everything when we talked with the police," he protested.

"I want to hear it from you . . . to me," she nodded and looked up into his handsome face.

"It won't change anything."

"I know that. But you've been spying on me for seven weeks without my knowledge, and you've been looking for Charlie over three years."

Before he could say a word, she stood and retrieved the two vases, one yellow from the kitchen table, the other burgundy from her bedroom dresser, and gave them to him. "No more listening in on me," she insisted. "It's time that you tell me everything." She hoped by her tone that he knew how serious she considered the situation.

Wade nodded. "The wires in these vases were Danny's idea," he said as he set the vases aside.

She smiled. "I figured that out on my own."

Wade pulled her down beside him and stared deep into her eyes. Nicole studied his expression with all the love that she felt in her heart. To her amazement, she could see that love reflecting back at her through his blue, blue eyes. Immediately, the tension she'd felt over the last two months was released between them. Finally, there would be no more secrets.

After kissing her forehead, Wade said, "When Sharelle was lying in the hospital, fighting for her life, our family stayed by her side, taking turns so that she was never alone. We talked to her, rubbed lotion on her feet and legs, read the daily newspaper to her. One afternoon about six weeks into this vigil, we were all gathered around her, talking, almost pretending that she was awake and participating. It started to get dark, and one by one, the rest of the family went to dinner. I stayed behind. Sharelle had been in a coma all that time, and the doctors couldn't tell us when she would come out of it."

"It must have been horrible," Nicole said. "But you were alone with her when she came to?"

"I was holding her hand," Wade nodded. "Suddenly, these enormous tears started spilling from her eyes. I reached for some tissue and dried them. She grabbed my wrist and whispered, *Wade. You have to stop them.* For a moment, I didn't know who she meant. I asked who did this to her. Then, she released my wrist, lifted her other hand and pointed to her ring finger. She said, *Charlie, he took my ring.* As quickly as she had gained consciousness, she fell back into a deep sleep and didn't wake up for three more weeks. When she did, she had no memory of what she'd told me. I took the information to the police, but they said it was considered hearsay unless she told them herself. Her words to me were inadmissible. The problem is, she's never told the same thing to anyone else. Since that day, I have considered it my personal responsibility to find Charlie Blaugh – whom you know as Charlie Hackett – and to prove the truth about him. That's why I came here."

"So, all this time, it's all been a charade." Nicole whispered, tears forming in her eyes.

"Unless you call this a charade," he said, plunking the engagement ring Charlie had given her into Nicole's hand.

"Where did you get this?" she gasped, recognizing it immediately.

"It belonged to my grandmother, who bequeathed it to Sharelle, her oldest grandchild. Charlie stole it from Sharelle the night he and his brothers left her to die in that ravine."

"Charlie said it was his mother's," she sniffled and wiped her nose on a tissue.

"I recognized it the moment I saw it on your hand. But how could I ask you to give it back? Instead, I took it from beneath your kitchen table, the night Charlie knocked it out of your hand. I hope you can forgive me." His bold blue eyes brightened with moisture.

"Of course," she said, stroking his face with her hand. "I never even missed it. And I don't want it. Please, give it back to Sharelle."

Wade smiled. "I will," he nodded.

"Now, tell me about you and Danny," she insisted.

Wade frowned momentarily, then seemed to gather courage as he began his explanations about her brother. "I gave Danny the money, as you'll recall. I didn't know much about Ella, nor Danny's devotion to her. He seemed so eager, at first, to take my money, that I worried if Danny had a gambling debt, but it turns out he doesn't. I've since looked into Danny's affairs, about Ella and everything. I believe him." Wade shrugged convincingly.

"Then, how did I come into the picture?" she persisted.

"When Danny met Ella's mother, Grace, he learned she is a paraplegic. Grace and Sharelle both do volunteer work for *Paraplegics Anonymous*. Grace introduced Danny to Sharelle, who introduced me to Danny.

"One day last August, I brought Sharelle to the hospital in Denver for her hydrotherapy, and when she was done, we were just leaving when we ran into Ella and Danny, who were just arriving with Grace. While they waited for Grace's hydrotherapy session to conclude, the four of us, Sharelle, Ella and Danny and I went down to the hospital cafeteria for lunch. Danny likes to brag about his marine biologist sister, and when he heard that I, too, am a marine biologist, he pulled a photo out of his wallet. It was one of you and Charlie after a successful salmon fishing trip."

Nicole nodded, remembering how much Charlie protested having that photo taken. It was the only one she had, and she'd given a copy of it to Danny.

Continuing his story, Wade said, "I recognized Charlie straight away. Sharelle asked to see the photo and I hesitated because I knew she would recognize him, too. Danny didn't understand my hesitation. He took the photo from me and plunked it down on the table in front of Sharelle, unaware that Charlie was the one who had crippled her."

"How did she react?" asked Nicole, sickened at how it must have made Sharelle feel.

"The color drained from her face. She stared for only a moment, then she went ballistic and screamed at Danny to take it away. She was positively hysterical. Danny didn't know what he'd done to offend her, so while Ella stayed with Sharelle and comforted her, I took Danny into the conservatory and told him what I knew for sure about Charlie, and how I knew you were in grave danger. After I expressed my concerns to Danny, he told me he already suspected

Charlie would abuse you. He had already gone to Charlie and warned him to stay away. But Charlie took that as a personal challenge. From what we've both learned, Charlie was only after your stocks, bonds and real estate. He drained my cousin's finances and beat her up a few times, so she left him. But he came back for revenge, and look what happened. Neither of us could let that happen to you."

"So you wanted to drive a wedge between me and Charlie by pretending to be interested in me?"

"Yes," he admitted. "And no. I admit that I drove Charlie away from you, but I never pretended about how much you attracted me. It astounded me to discover I was so attracted to you."

"Was?" she asked, still an edge of concern in her heart.

"Let me rephrase. I knew from the moment I met you that I would never be the same. My desire to protect Danny's innocent sister became a passion that consumed me. I could let nothing and no one harm you, and I probably went a little overboard in my zeal to ensure your safety. I fell in love with you, Nicole. And I had just about given up hope that you might feel the same."

She gazed into his eyes, loving his words, loving him more than she could say. Wade seemed to wait for her response to his declaration, but she let him wonder for a little while so she could assimilate all the information she had taken in during the past twenty-four hours.

Satisfied that he really did love her, which was clearly evident by the concern on his face, she whispered, "You made me love you, Wade, that day on the beach . . . but I knew you were hiding something from me, and I was concerned what kind of man you were, to take advantage of my brother like you did."

"That's where you're wrong, Nicole. I never *loaned* Danny a dime. I gave him some money, but not nearly as much as you think. It was part of my investment to bring Charlie to justice, and in my opinion, money well spent. Danny's stocks and bonds, the real estate, that was all an act from both of us. I don't own half your property, Danny still does."

"But the documentation, Wade. I saw the real estate contract," Nicole persisted.

"We destroyed all the paper work right after we were convinced you thought it was all real. Nicole, I knew Charlie was only after your assets, so Danny and I planned to strip you of at least Danny's share. This would throw Charlie off-base, and we hoped that if he knew he couldn't get everything, Charlie might lose interest."

"You're making Danny out to be a saint, but you mustn't forget that he did steal my mama's jewelry." Nicole still could not believe her brother had changed so much.

"Danny wanted Charlie away from you as badly as I did. Like Danny told you that day you went horseback riding. Danny learned his lesson the hard way. He repented and put his life in order."

"So he owes you nothing?" she asked, surprised to hear of Danny's role in all the deception.

Wade shook his head, a glint of honor in his eyes. "Absolutely nothing. It was a gift. And worth every penny to ensure your safety."

"Then why was he paying you back?" she demanded.

"Because he truly has changed," Wade persisted. "Danny wanted to pay me back for the little that I gave him in our attempt to convince you that he had sold everything to me."

Amazed and relieved, Nicole leaned in closer to Wade and thrilled to his rubbing her back in a tantalizing manner. Then she remembered, and tapped the yellow vase meaningfully. "Wait a minute. You were listening in on my conversation with Danny the day we went horseback riding?"

"Sorry. Yes."

"And you still thought I was pregnant?"

"Mmm. No. But it made a good ruse, didn't it?" He lifted and lowered his eyebrows twice, then gave her a teasing grin.

Pulling away, Nicole hit him in the arm. Hard. "Wade! What a way to win a girl's heart," she complained.

"It worked, though. Didn't it?" he asked, giving her a hungry look that melted her all the way to her toes.

In answer to his question, Nicole nodded her head, and pulled him closer to her where she lingered, lip to lip, a very long time.

When she finally let him up for air, Wade winked. "Does this mean you plan to give me a key to our grandpa's house?"

"Does this mean you intend to marry me?" she countered with a question of her own.

They stared intensely for several long minutes, Nicole wondering if she had been too bold, too forward to have asked such a question.

"As a matter of fact," he said at last, pulling a velvet ring box from his pocket, "I planned to ask you up at the camp . . . ." He left the suggestion dangling before her and opened the box to reveal a beautiful gold and diamond ring.

Nicole laughed and threw her arms around him, giving him a delicious smile, then she kissed him longingly, deeply, satisfyingly.

When she finally let him up for air, he whispered huskily against her lips, "I like your answer."

Epilogue:

Claude and Margo Browning recently celebrated their twentieth wedding anniversary where Margo announced they were expecting the first hatchlings of domesticated crabs in their successful automated Dungeness crab farm.

Matt and Catherine Hemsley retired from their farmers' market and turned the business over to their son, his wife and their seven children. They still travel to Yuma, Arizona every winter to escape from the hectic world of grandchildren. Catherine has found amazing success with her forty caliber Glock, teaching babyboomers the art of self-defense.

Charlie and Devin were convicted of six counts of attempted murder and one murder in the first degree. They are currently serving life sentences without the possibility of parole in the Oregon State Penitentiary. Their fleet of boats were confiscated, and all but the smallest of them were found to be stolen. Weapons and evidence seized in the search linked the brothers to three additional murders in other coastal areas, for which they were subsequently convicted. While serving lifetime prison sentences, their duties include digging ditches . . . six days a week.

At Charlie's insistence, Bo's ashes were taken aboard the only boat he ever owned, a small wooden trawler called *Rip Tide*. Charlie intended to hire a captain to scatter Bo's ashes at sea, but he wasted all his money on legal fees. Unfortunately, the *Rip Tide* was declared derelict by the United States Coast Guard. It was seized, towed five miles out in the Pacific Ocean and deliberately sunk. The sealed plastic container of human ash went down with the boat, so Bo was considered a total loss.

Daniel Travis received his master's degree, married Ella Schoonaker, and went on to get his doctorate. Today he is president of Travis & Schoonaker Pharmaceuticals. He lives in an upscale Denver area with two and a half children and a dog. Danny, Ella and their family visit coastal Oregon twice a year where they vacation in the home his grandfather built.

Nicole and Wade got married in December, the day after she received her doctorate in marine biology. Occasionally, Wade teaches at MIC, but he prefers acting. His new role is called Fatherhood . . . to his and Nicole's *mischievous* triplets. Meanwhile, Nicole teaches seminars at colleges and universities all along the West Coast, where her textbook, *Cancer Magister*, is required reading for all marine biology students. Wade and Nicole built a seven-bedroom home at Grandpa's Pines, just in case she gets pregnant a *second* time. They spend their evenings and weekends together studying wild life along the beach . . . theirs!

Brubaker still shows up the third of the month in Bandon-by-the-Sea to collect his social security check and do his marketing. He can't understand why the police insist on periodic sweeps of his property. They say they're looking for a dead body. This explanation only confuses Brubaker, who finally confessed, "I ain't killed a bear outa' season . . . not fer days and days!"

Sherry Ann Miller is the proud mother of seven children and their choice spouses, and twenty-six grandchildren. She sails through life loving her husband and family, writing fiction and non-fiction, researching her family history, crocheting and studying marine life on the beach near her home. Sherry Ann has finally accumulated enough sailing hours to earn her Captain's License . . . if she can just gather enough courage to take the USCG test. She and her hubby spend several weeks each summer navigating their sailing vessel, *Shoosey-Q*, through northwest waters.

For Sherry Ann, being under sail is one of life's most exhilarating experiences. That . . . and surviving Motherhood!

Introducing Sherry Ann Miller's five-book *Gift Series*

You're going to love all five novels in Sherry Ann Miller's popular *Gift Series.* The *Gift Series* will take you on the individual sojourns of Kayla Dawn Allen and the five men who have influenced her life for good: the Sparkleman boys, Ed, Abbot and Tom, who grew up with Kayla on the *Bar M Ranch*; and the seafaring Clark twins, Joshua (who loves Kayla more than life itself) and Hans (who is always one step behind in finding his soul-mate). Each novel will plunge you into a miraculous, spine-tingling journey about life, love, heartache and triumphant joy. If you've a thirst for adventure, drama, action and romance, try all five novels in Sherry Ann's award-winning *Gift Series:*

One Last Gift Kayla is rescued from her own scientific disposition, her misguided infatuation with Ed Sparkleman, and even more desperate and dangerous elements in *One Last Gift.* Kayla's remarkable journey, from her sailboat in San Diego to her childhood home high in the Uinta Mountains, finds her facing many obstacles, until she finally discovers God's mighty miracles are all around her. At the satisfying conclusion, only one question remains, "What about Ed?'"

An Angel's Gift Ed Sparkleman meets his match when Alyssa drops in on the *Bar M Ranch* (literally!) and disrupts his life forever. As ranch foreman, Ed is responsible for keeping his men in order, but with Alyssa around, all the ranch hands begin to act oddly out of character . . .especially Ed. Is Alyssa truly ***An Angel's Gift*** sent straight to him from heaven? If so, what about his brother, Abbot?

The Tyee's Gift Set in the picturesque Pacific Northwest, adventure meets Abbot Sparkleman when he discovers the greatest archaeological site of the century and falls in love with the beautiful and mysterious Bekah. ***The Tyee's Gift*** will bring tears of laughter, joy and heartache while Abbot learns where much is given, much is required.

Charity's Gift Debuting in August 2006. When Hans comes face to face with a ferocious shark, it strikes less fear than vivacious and attractive Charity, who throws his heart into a spiraling nose-dive deep in the Pacific Ocean. The only way he can salvage their crumbling romance is to find her missing father, who's been absent from Charity's life for more than twenty years. ***Charity's Gift*** will touch your heart forever.

The Refiner's Gift The fifth and final novel in the ***Gift Series*** is now in progress, and answers the worrisome question, "What about Tom?" who was accused of a vicious crime in **One Last Gift**, six years ago. Tom Sparkleman has not yet escaped the consequences of that crime. The miracles that await him in **The Refiner's Gift** will astound everyone.

The series can be read out of sequence without losing continuity.

Sherry Ann Miller's two-book **Warwick Saga**

Search for the Bark Warwick begins with the stowaway who interrupts and changes John's life forever. It concludes with John's desperate search for his captive son. This historical novel, based loosely on a true story, is a stirring tale of surprise, compassion, love and tenacious devotion to family. The story of a genuine hero in 1630's England, **Search for the Bark Warwick** will keep you on the edge of your seat, and leave you begging for more.

Search for the Warwick II proves once and for all why Sherry Ann Miller is known as the writer of miracles. The absorbing sequel, **Search for the Warwick II**, concludes the search for John Dunton's son who is enslaved in 1630's Algeria, where a generous reward has been offered for

John's capture. Now, John must not only find Thomas, he must avoid recapture while he and his devoted crew attempt to outsail and outmaneuver a horde of evil pirates. Nothing else matters to John or his men . . . not even their own lives.

The Warwick Saga is complete in two novels and should be read in sequence.

Sherry Ann Miller's beloved
Gardenia Sunrise

A stand-alone novel, *Gardenia Sunrise* is the emotional journey of Brandje Fulton. Brandje flees to her villa on the west coast of France, hoping to prepare herself emotionally and spiritually to meet God after she learns that she has cancer. Her plans are altered when a hot-headed American arrives for his annual holiday at the villa, unaware that his reservation has been canceled. Brandje's story is a heart-thumping, inspirational romance of the finest kind.